1

2

PRINCESS IN THE POLICE STATION:
A Tale of Little Anne Mowbray

By J.P. Reedman

AUTHOR'S NOTE: Some of the figures in the 20th century sections of this work are real people. For this reason, I have changed their names, to protect their privacy and that of their families, and because, as a fiction writer, I can only guess at their thoughts and feelings when the true events of Anne Mowbray's finding and reburial unfolded in 1964/5

East London in December. Bleak. Cold. Haunting.

Icy winds skirled through the shells of derelict buildings, howling around the craters left by the aerial bombardments of The Blitz. Sleet streamed from a bruised purple sky, while on the horizon rays of the early sunset stabbed through the tiered clouds like swords, staining the domed turrets of the Tower of London crimson and turning the sluggish ribbon of the Thames to blood.

Not far from the ancient fortress, workman Bob Potter drove his excavator forward into the gloom of a building clearance site, eager to shunt away as much rubble as possible before home time. His gloveless hands were freezing, his fingers almost numb with cold and in danger of getting chilblains—he wanted nothing more than to clock off and head home for his tea before spending the night watching the telly with the wife. Only a short while now and the feeble remains of daylight would die and Mr Biggs, the foreman, would arrive from the other site he was managing and call an official halt to work.

Driven by the happy promise of the day's finish, Bob revved the excavator's engine and drove up and over the uneven ground, mounded with bricks and rubble and coils of twisted barbed wire. A wall reared up, slightly different in character to the rest of the tumbled stones—solid, grey, big blocks. Digging had revealed it only that morning. It was sturdy but it had to go; the whole area was marked for urban renewal.

The excavator's bucket dipped on its long arm as the boom swung round, monstrous in the twilight with its edges rimmed by metal spikes that resembled a dragon's teeth. The engine roared and the bucket's spikes snapped at a section of the newly uncovered wall. A puff of dust wafted into the air, ghost-like, as a section of stonework began to crumble.

Suddenly Bob felt the whole vehicle shake, jerking and juddering as if grabbed by an unseen hand and shaken. The digger lurched forward, the grousers on its tracks failing to stop its momentum as it slid over unstable heaped mounds of dirt and rubble.

Unable to determine what exactly had happened and fearing he was losing control of his vehicle, Bob frantically tried to reverse, to no avail—the digger was still bucking like a wild horse, and earth and stones were spraying wildly from under the tracks.

Swearing, he slammed on the brakes and killed the engine. The forward plunge of the excavator ceased, but he could not go backwards as the arm and boom were leaning at an awkward angle. He squinted through the grimy windscreen and then whistled. The bucket was hanging through the hole he had made in the old wall. But that wasn't the issue. It was what was under the breach. Darkness. An unknown cavern seemed to have opened up in the ground.

Shakily, Bob climbed out of the cab and picked his way over the rough ground towards the dangling bucket.

"What's the matter?" His workmate, Terry Hanrahan, who had been digging on the far side of the site, ploughed through the twilight murk, his face mud-splotched and cold beneath his hardhat. "Why are you stopping, Bob? Something wrong?"

"I—I...*Something* has happened." Bob nodded in the direction of his excavator, leaning awkwardly on the spoil, its dark bulk silhouetted against the faded sky. "I don't know what, though. Remember that wall we dug out this morning, the one with different coloured stone to the rest of the building? The one where the foundations were way down deep? Well, when I went to knock it over, the bucket struck straight through the wall and then the whole bloomin' digger tipped...For a second, I thought I was going to fall into a bottomless pit or that the excavator was going to tip over. I need to take a closer look at what's there before making another move. Can't say I'm sure the ruddy digger is stable even now."

"I'll come with you," offered Terry. "Safer if there's two of us. I'm pretty much done in my section. Just waiting for the final whistle to go home."

Together, the two workmen inched over the wreckage of fallen masonry on the site. Bricks rolled and rattled; wind shrilled between the gaunt skeletons of standing walls. It almost felt as if they were entering a war zone—a dangerous area with booby traps hidden at every turn.

In the grey chunk of wall stretched a lightless crater. The excavator bucket dangled into the gap on its long boom.

Terry took a few steps closer, trying to peer around the edge of the hole. He gazed down…into what appeared to be an underground chamber. He leaned over, striving to get a better look, but detritus rattled under his work boots, making him almost lose his footing. Uttering a few choice profanities, he stumbled back to Bob's side.

"I think you've hit an underground cellar or bunker, mate," he said. "Maybe from an old warehouse? Lots of 'em round here once."

"The stonework I hit looks too substantial to come from a modern warehouse." Bob nodded towards the ruinous wall. "*That* looks like it was made to last centuries. I *do* know there used to be an old chapel hereabouts. St Trinity's. Took a direct hit from a bomb in 1940 and was destroyed. So, who knows? Could be part of that."

"Church crypt then?" Terry's eyes widened, becoming black hollows in the twilight. "Christ, we could have some unhappy relatives blaming us for digging up Aunt Agatha."

"Don't think they buried people at Trinity's, not in recent years anyway. I remember seeing the place as a lad. A plain church, with a little spire and white walls. Closed years before and all boarded up. My granddad said they once had a human head on display there…a severed head in a glass case!"

"You're having me on, mate!" exclaimed Terry with a nervous laugh. "A severed head?"

Bob folded his arms. "It's true, I'm not telling porkies. They thought it was some bloke executed by Henry VIII or some other vicious sod back in them days. The head was taken to St Botolph's when Trinity closed. Don't know anymore, though. History was never my thing; I wasn't no swot in school. I know a few dates like 1066, but that's it, I'm afraid."

"Still could be dead folk here," shrugged Terry. "Maybe from earlier than St Trinity's. I remember overhearing a tour guide saying there was an old convent around here...hundreds of years old. Nuns of St. Clare, and that's why we have a St. Clare's Street nearby."

"Heard that too. The name 'Minories' also has something to do with it. Well, there's only one thing left to do," said Bob. "Let me grab a torch and we'll have a proper look in the hole."

Bob hurried to the excavator's cab and brought out a Britram Empire flashlight. He flicked it on. A bright white beam slashed into the murkiness.

Bob approached the wall taking one careful step after the other. The beam of his torch danced over the sturdy stonework—limestone, maybe? Definitely not modern or Victorian brick like he was used to seeing from the ruined warehouses on other parts of the site. This was old eroded stone and close up showed some signs of tooling.

As he reached the fissure in the stone and shone the light down as best he could, he became sure it was a crypt of some sort, just as Terry had suggested. Although he didn't have enough room to angle the torch properly, he could see a greenish, damp floor, and a graceful stone arch. The chamber spewed out the rank scent of dampness and age.

"It's some kind of vault all right," Bob said to his companion.

"What should we do?" Terry shuffled up behind, trying to peer over his shoulder.

"Well, Mr Biggs will arrive soon to sign us off for the day...but we probably should try to find out what we've discovered before he gets here. Biggs won't be too pleased if he finds us standing around with our hands in our pockets. You know what he's like, grumpy git."

Terry was still striving to see what was in the underground chamber. "Dammit, the bucket's in the way. Can we get in there and have a proper look, do you think? Take a bit more wall down?"

Bob looked dubious. "I'd want to be sure it wouldn't collapse and kill us. Could be unstable. Some of these places round here weren't sound even before the Luftwaffe dumped bombs on them"

"Shall we give it a little test?" Terry hefted a chunk of broken concrete from the floor of a destroyed warehouse and flung it at the stone wall with all his strength. It thudded against the exterior stonework, making a hollow, echoing noise deep below, in what seemed the very bowels of the earth.

"Eerie," murmured Bob nervously as the sound died away. "The sound of those echoes." Hairs stood up on the back of his neck.

"I am fairly certain it's not about to collapse." Terry pressed a hand on the wall where his missile had struck, testing his weight against it. "I gave it quite a blow. Whoever built this knew what he was doing." A sudden boyish enthusiasm in his eyes, he glanced over at Bob. "You never know what might be lying in there, mate. Could be a second King Tut's tomb! Might make us rich as lords!""

Bob gave a derisive snort. "Tut's tomb? Here in England? Not likely, matey. It looks a bit fancy but let's not let imagination run away with us. Yeah, yeah, my first thought when I looked in was a church crypt. But I ain't no historian. Could just as easily be an old sewer. Or just a cellar. Ha, the best we might do is find a few bottles of vintage wine down there."

"I still think it's a burial crypt. Gut feeling. As I said before, there was a convent here hundreds of years ago." Terry grabbed the torch from Bob and muscled him aside, sending shafts of light spinning across the surface of the structure. "Look at the shape. Rises to a peak there. Bloody hell, I am pretty sure I even see an old mason's mark! I am guessing this place *is* old, though how old I can't say any more than you can. Come on, Bob, don't be so stuffy. We should at least have a decent peek inside that hole you made. And you were the one who said we should look busy for when Biggs gets here!"

Bob was still not convinced it was wise it to proceed into the vault but he was not going to look foolish or cowardly in front of his younger workmate. "I meant assess the place from the outside…but go on, then if you're so keen." He tipped his chin in the direction of the cracked wall. "You first, my lad. Since it was your idea to go in."

Terry cast him an impish grin and knelt beside the bucket, beating his gloved fist on the edge of the fissure in the wall in an attempt to dislodge a few more stones to allow him passage. More hollow booms echoed through the unseen underworld below. The stones. However, remained firmly in place.

"Not big enough!" he shouted over his shoulder. "Do you want to try reversing the excavator again?"

Bob shook his head and scowled. "That might well bring the whole structure down. The stone below waist level seems sound enough but I'm not so sure about the roof. Getting hit by the bucket might well have weakened or fractured it. Instead, how about I get a sledgehammer to open the gap a bit further?"

"Sounds like a plan."

Returning to the excavator's cab, Bob unlatched his toolbox again and removed his trusty sledgehammer. *I must be mad*, he thought, but he could not deny that excitement was growing in his heart. A sense of wonder, a desire for adventure that he hadn't felt since he was a lad. Terry's enthusiasm was indeed infectious.

Hammer in hand, he stumped over the spoil heaps and tumbled stones to whatever he had unwittingly unearthed. His toecaps hit against the old stonework and, despite his stubbed toes, he breathed a sigh of relief—Terry was right, it *did* seem sound and probably would hold, at least for a cursory inspection.

His workmate was already kneeling at the lip of the hole, using his hands to shovel broken chunks from around the edges of the bucket. Knees creaking as he sank down uncomfortably, Bob squatted next to him and began loosening up masonry with the sledgehammer.

*Bang…bang…bang…*The noise of each hammer blow reverberated through the unknown spaces below.

As the two men worked and the daylight deteriorated even further, they became aware that they had an audience. Several builders from the other half of the site were now standing by the excavator, alongside a rag-tag band of local school children who had sneaked onto the site as they often did, against site and school rules.

"Eh, Joe!" Bob roared at one of the watching men, waving his arm. "Don't just stand there. Get them kids off the site. When the foreman comes down, and he'll be here soon, he won't be happy…"

"Hey, mister, we're not hurting nuffin," called out a snub-faced lad in a battered school cap. "We just want to see."

"Yeah," cried his fellow, a short, stocky boy with a cowlick in the fringe of his glossy dark hair. "We were goin' home but saw the digger nearly fall over. We were excited, like. Thought maybe someone might have been 'urt and we could watch…."

"You're a charmer, ain't you," said Bob, sarcastically, "That was *me* in the excavator, thank you very much!" Little scrotes, speaking to him like that! No discipline and no matters. He'd have had a right thumping from his old mum if he'd cheeked an adult in such a way!

"So what's down there, mister?" Cowlick slinked towards the crevice in the wall like an eager weasel.

"You stay right there!" Bob ordered, glaring and holding up a hand in front of the boy like a copper directing traffic. "You're not supposed to be here. It's too dangerous for you little toerags."

Cowlick stopped in his tracks, but neither he nor his mate looked upset by being chastised…nor did they back off and leave, although their less gobby school chums backed off a few paces, ready to run for it if chased.

"What's down in that old hole, mister? Treasure?" Snub-nose sauntered over. "Looks a bit boring, but maybe there's a monster, like in one of my comic books. It crawled under London, came up the sewers…"

"Don't be stupid" Bob growled, rolling his eyes in irritation. "There's no such thing as monsters…except you lot, that is! Now get off with you, your mothers will be wondering where you are."

"What if we don't wanna go?" asked Snub-nose impudently. He took off his cap and scratched furiously at his Beatles mop-top haircut.

Bob gave the little yob a hard look. If that was *his* son, he'd drag him to the nearest barber for a haircut and then wash his gobby little mouth out with soap. "We'll call the old Bill if we have to."

"Yeah? How? Time you find a copper, we'll have long scarpered……"

Bob gritted his teeth at the boy's insolence and took a step in his direction that was meant to look menacing but lost its impact as he stumbled over a stone.

"Come on, mate!" Terry gesturing to him. "Ignore them little yobos; they'll soon lose interest. Joe should be warding them off anyways…if he'd stop gawking. He's as bad as they are!"

Scowling, Bob turned back to the hole. *Bang*…The hammer struck another stone and a jagged line appeared between it and its fellow. He struck it again. Both stones broke loose and tumbled into the chamber below with a loud noise. This was followed by another and then another. The schoolchildren began to cheer.

Terry leaned forward, poking his head into the widened gap. "I'm beginning to see something…*Whoah*!"

He grabbed the torch and shone it into the ever-widening hole. "Bloody hell, what's that down there?"

"Told you it'd be a monster!" shouted Snub-nose, who was creeping uncomfortably close and earwigging on the two demolition workers. His yell was followed by a burst of childish laughter from Cowlick and the rest of the rag-tag urchins.

Bob ignored the children and hurried to Terry's side, staring down into the hole. He saw the green-stained floor he'd first noted stretching away, a second arch, then a third, a battered stone pillar supporting the roof. "Looks pretty complete, wouldn't like to guess the age, but I'm guessing 'old.' You going in first?"

"Just try and stop me. Finders-keepers if I *do* discover treasure." Terry swung his legs over the edge and pushed himself forward, dropping several feet to the damp, slimy floor. He began waving the torch around, showing the extent of the chamber's vaulted roof…and then, suddenly, he uttered a strangled scream. "*Jesus*! What the hell is that!"

The torch fell from his fingers with a clatter and rolled on the ground. Light beams mingled with shadows bounced wildly all over the walls as Terry snatched up the fallen torch, before staggering back from whatever he had spotted in the crypt.

Bob stared at his mate, open-mouthed in surprise. In all the years they had worked together, he had never seen Terry white as a sheet and shaking. Although good-natured, Terry was no push-over; he was a tough bloke, born and bred from Irish migrants in the East End. But now he looked as if he had seen a ghost.

Apprehensive but intrigued, the older man forced his way through the breach in the wall and jumped the last few feet into the unearthed crypt. Staggering over to Terry, he grabbed the torch, which now hung limply from the other man's hand, and shone it around the chamber.

Illuminated by the thin, yellowish rays sent out by the torch, he could now identify what exactly had spooked his workmate.

Against the dripping, mouldering wall lay a coffin. It was not very big—not large enough to hold a full-grown adult—so he presumed it must hold the remains of a young child. The coffin was vaguely anthropomorphic in shape, mirroring the human form of the body it encased. It appeared to be fashioned from thick lead.

"Hell, I honestly didn't expect that." Bob walked over to Terry and clapped him on the shoulder. "But I don't think whoever's in that coffin is able to hurt us, so you needn't look so scared, mate."

"I-I'm not scared," scowled Terry, embarrassed by his loss of composure. "Gave me a bit of a shock, is all. You'd have been the same if you came down 'ere first."

"Well, now we're both here, let's have a gander. See what's what." Bob lifted the torch and began to slowly walk around the room, Terry close on his heels. Examining the stonework in close proximity, Bob guessed it might be some kind of chalk rubble. The chamber wasn't very high, the ceiling perhaps only about half a foot above his head, nor was it all that wide, although it had a greater length. The rubble was moss-splotched and moisture-laden, the air foul. The place was claustrophobic and he bit back a wave of nausea; he had never liked enclosed spaces. Over on the far wall was a bricked-up doorway with a tall, pointed arch, no doubt once leading to further buried structures.

"What do we do now?" asked Terry as they finished the inspection of their surroundings and gathered next to the tiny coffin.

"I think we should get this out." Bob nodded towards the lead sarcophagus. "And then we get a copper. Or the museum. Or…or…I don't know who, just someone who knows more about these things than we do."

The men retreated from the coffin and clambered back out of the hole. Now an even larger crowd had formed—not just the rest of the workmen, who had all downed tools, but more schoolboys and girls, and even the staff exiting nearby offices for the night.

"Oh, we heard you found a mummy!" said a young office temp wearing a fashionable mini-skirt and heels. Her dyed blonde hair towered in a lacquered beehive. "Is it true? Can we see it?"

Terry shook his head at her. "No, sorry. Off-limits."

"If it's true, that's *disgusting*!" mumbled a large matronly woman who was pushing a crying infant in a pram. "Digging up the dead like that. You should have more respect."

A man in a bowler hat, carrying a brolly under his arm, huffed at the woman. "The workmen found it by accident. What do you expect them to do? Leave the whole place a literal bombsite, a place for vagrants and criminals to lurk in, just because some mouldy old skeletons might be buried below?"

The woman gasped in rage, her fleshy face turning a florid pink. She looked like she was seriously considering ramming her baby's pram into the bowler-hatted businessman.

Fearful that tensions would erupt into arguments or even a full-on brawl, some of the site workmen finally stepped in and began ushering the onlookers off the site. They went from bemusement to irritation as the snoopers argued or dawdled, but eventually they chased the gawkers away, though some of the most persistent loitered across the road in the newly fallen darkness, watching to see what would happen next.

Bob and Terry fetched a large, sturdy chain from the site's storeroom and returned to the burial vault. Kneeling, they wrapped the links around the leg area of the coffin where it was narrowest.

"Do you think this is a good idea?" Terry asked, his breath a white haze before his lips in the coolness of the chamber. "What…what if it comes open while it is being lifted?"

"We can't leave it here. Turn your eyes away for an instant and someone would be in here nicking it."

"Maybe…but it's bloody heavy!"

Bob's bushy eyebrows lifted. "You really think that'd stop 'em? You're having a laugh, mate. No, we need to get the coffin out tonight before it gets too dark and put it into the hands of the proper authorities."

Grabbing the loose end of the chain, he fastened it around the arm of the excavator, yanking on it to test that it was tight enough. "All good."

Bob scrambled back out of the crypt into the outside world. The local children were still milling in the street along with a few new unsavoury types. Ignoring them, he climbed into the cab of the excavator and started the engine. Carefully he began to reverse, careful not to go too fast. For a few heart-stopping moments, it lurched back and forth, tracks seeking purchase in the building debris, but this time he was luckier than before; while he was attaching the chain to the coffin, his work colleagues up above had dug out some of the rubble piles and placed boards down to make a flatter, safer surface. The vehicle rolled back with an almighty roar from the engine.

Emerging from the vault, Terry was using the torch to track the progress of the lead coffin. "It's moving…it's coming out!" he shouted over the rumble of the excavator. "Careful now! Careful!"

Bob continued to reverse, his brow furrowed in concentration. The boom jerked up, straining at the sky, and a few seconds later, the coffin appeared, dangling in mid-air and hanging upside down, resembling a grisly pinata in some monstrous child's game. There were shouts and cheers from the nearby watchers, who clearly hoped the ancient lead would give way and the coffin contents spill out before their hopeful, ghoulish eyes.

As Bob lowered the digger's arm and set the sarcophagus down on the ground, the foreman, Fred Biggs, arrived on site. He stared around, nonplussed by the crowds gathered under the newly turned-on streetlights.

"What's going on here?" he asked gruffly. "It's like a bloody circus."

Bob climbed from his seat in the excavator. "Something's happened, Mr…"

"I can bloody well see that." Bigg's brows lowered to almost Neanderthal levels. "What is it? Spit it out."

Bob gestured towards the coffin, pitifully small and badly battered, which now lay flat on the ground beside the excavator.

Mr Biggs' eyes bulged in their sockets. "Is that what I think it is?"

"Yes, sir. It is."

"Jesus Christ," said the foreman.

The press turned up next; word of the find had run riot through London's streets. Camera flash-bulbs popped in the gloom, lighting up the pathetic sarcophagus, which had now been hauled upright to get the best angles. Bob, stiff and uncomfortable in his muddy work trousers and jacket, stood by it wearing a rigid fixed grin, half-blinded by the camera flashes and feeling like a fish out of water.

At least old curmudgeon Biggs was no longer glaring as if he thought Bob and Terry and had committed some sort of crime. After his initial shock, the foreman seemed to be enjoying the publicity, talking to the reporters while cameras focussed on Bob and his macabre find. Terry had managed to slink off, the jammy git, repulsed by the idea of having his mug plastered all over tomorrow's papers.

Once the journos and press photographers began to lose interest and the other onlookers, bored by the lack of gold, jewels, or a visible mummy, vanished into the haze of car headlights and moving double-deckers, Fred Biggs turned to Bob and coughed. "I'll take over now. You can be off home, Potter."

"Right you are, sir. Glad for this day to end, to be honest, but what are you going to do with...*it*?" Bob nodded towards the coffin propped against the digger.

"Take it to the Old Bill, of course," said Fred Biggs with a sniff. "Come on, Potter, the rest of you lazy sods too. Between you all, you can drag it to the roadside and stand guard. I'll get my car."

Biggs strode off to where his vehicle was parked, while the few remaining workmen on the Minories site gathered around the dented sarcophagus like a muddy, hard-hatted ring of mourners.

The foreman returned shortly, leaping from behind the wheel of his Land Rover and yanking the back door open. "Get it in," he ordered. "Quickly, I don't have all night. It's bloody freezing out here and there might be some other nosy cranks ready to cause a commotion if it's spotted."

The workmen jumped to attention, manhandling the coffin over to Fred Bigg's vehicle and pushing it into the back with much straining and shoving. Bob, lifting the head of the sarcophagus, fancied he could feel *contents* moving around within and his stomach began to churn. He did not want to think about what might be happening to the disturbed corpse inside the lead casing.

Finally, the macabre burden was loaded into the car. Fred Biggs slammed the Safari door shut and rubbed his hands together. "I'll be off then. I expect you lot all in nice and early tomorrow. I imagine the Fleet Street crew will be back again, along with other curious folks. We don't need any of them poking and prying…and getting into trouble. You might need to put up some barricades and play the part of security guards."

Instructions given, Biggs jumped into the driver's seat of the Land Rover and revved the engine noisily. Bob and the others moved back as the car lurched out into the steady stream of traffic, causing a barrage of blaring horns.

A strange melancholy descended over Bob Potter as the Land Rover disappeared into the press of vehicles. "Good journey to you, whoever you are…*were*," he murmured under his breath, and then he too slipped away into the night, his part in the discovery of the coffin over.

It was a quiet night in the Leman Street police station—so far. Paperwork rustled; cups of tea were brewed. "Too cold for the crims," grinned the newest young recruit. "Glad I'm not out on the beat tonight. Freeze my nose off."

"Pfft," snorted an older grey-haired copper as he thumbed the paperwork. "Enjoy it while you can, Davey. You'll be out there soon enough. And if you don't go out looking for trouble…Well, it often ends up on our doorstep anyway."

As if on cue, the front door crashed open. A middle-aged man wearing an expensive coat, his hair slicked flat from both Brill Cream and rain, barged into the station.

Instantly, the bobbies in the room snapped to attention, tea and biscuits swiftly hidden. The constable at the desk glanced up, clearing his throat. "How can we help you, sir?"

"I have a body…"

The coppers all stared at him, surprised by this unexpected admission.

"In my car…"

The young, spry policeman called Davey took a stride towards him, looking both alarmed and excited—would this be his first major arrest?

Fred Biggs lifted his hand, grinning sheepishly. "I didn't perhaps phrase that the right way. I am the foreman on the clearance site near that old, bombed-out church in Minories. Today, two of my men found an underground vault. About ten, eleven feet under. They broke through the wall and found a coffin inside. I took it away, as it was causing a nuisance with prying locals…"

"Sounds more like it's the Museum you need rather than the police," drawled the constable behind the desk, shuffling his papers.

Fred Biggs' lips pursed irritably. "That may well be the case, but it's long-gone closing time there. Are you going to help me or not? Old or new, it's still human remains."

"He's right; there must be a proper procedure for handling such things. And who knows, the coffin and its contents could be ancient—and valuable," said young Davey uncertainly, glancing to his fellow policemen for reassurance.

"Yes!" Biggs latched on to his hesitancy. "It may well be worth thousands of pounds, maybe more! Probably Roman, I'm guessing. Roman…They are always finding bits from them old Romans around here. Pots and nails and whatnot. If I leave the coffin in the car, some yobos are likely to make off with it overnight, and oh, wouldn't that be a terrible shame." He shook his head as if truly dejected at the thought, although it was clear to everyone in the room, he really only wanted to shove the responsibility onto someone else.

The Sergeant emerged from a side door, having caught a few snatches of the conversation from his office. "This is irregular, sir," he said to Biggs, "but if there's no helping it, we'll take the coffin off you and call the local Museum to pick it up first thing tomorrow."

A look of relief washed over Fred Biggs' face. "Good lads; I knew you'd come through for me. Now, could you come and help lift the damned thing out of my car? The coffin's lead and though it's not big, it's heavy and…" He pressed a hand against his lumbar spine and hunched over as if in pain. "I have a *very* bad back."

The Sergeant grimaced at Biggs' theatrics. "Don't worry, sir, we'll manage to lift without your help. Davey, stay on the desk and keep watch. The rest of you, go and get this sorted for Mr…Mr…"

"Biggs. Fred Biggs, foreman…"

"Mr Biggs. And…" The Sergeant glanced around at the other policemen. "The coffin is probably covered in muck. When you bring it in, try not to get the floor too dirty. It's just been washed!"

The coffin stood in the back office of the police station, leaning dejectedly against the wall. Jack Barnet, a retired Met copper who still kept a foot in the door by dealing with unexpected finds of human remains, stared down at it with interest, taking in its form and construction.

"So, what do you think, Jack? Roman?" asked the Sergeant, arms folded. "Eerie looking thing."

"Not Roman." Barnet shook his head. "I am guessing medieval. Before I came down to the station, I went to the library and had a look at the history of the area. St Trinity's was built on top of a much older building—a medieval nunnery, the Minories. Franciscan sisters of St. Clare."

"So, it's just some long-ago nun."

Jack Barnet shook his head again. "I doubt it, unless she was a dwarf. Look at the coffin's size! This is definitely a child's coffin, and to be alone in a vault with no other burials, I'd wager a pretty important child."

"But no proof."

"No. I had best call the Coroner and tell him that I am satisfied the burial is ancient and needs no further investigation."

The Sergeant ushered Barnet to the telephone and left the room as he dialled the Coroner's number. Once he had got through, he explained the circumstances of the find, his professional opinion of the age, and asked what would be the next step. As the Coroner answered, Jack's craggy face darkened and his lips pursed in irritation. "That's not much time," he said into the receiver. "Can't it be postponed for a few more days? No. Yes, I understand. Yes. Thank you. A good day to you too."

He placed the receiver back into the cradle and went to find the Sergeant. "Dammit. The Coroner told me that unless a bona fide claimant comes forward in twenty-four hours—which is highly unlikely—the coffin has to be reburied in a common grave in the City of London cemetery."

"Probably for the best," said the Sergeant. "After all, who's going to claim it after hundreds of years, and random bones turn up all over a city as old as this one."

"I am not convinced that the coffin belongs to just 'anyone', if you follow me, Sarge. I would have been happier to see the archaeologists take a look at what's inside. If you don't mind, I'd like another brief exam of the sarcophagus myself. See if there are any other clues."

"Whatever you want, Jack. You know what you're talking about. History's your speciality, not mine."

Barnet returned to the office where the coffin stood propped up, caked in layers of dry, flaking dirt. Kneeling beside it, he ran his hand over the lead surface, dinted and bumped, a combination of age wear and more recent damage that had happened when it was unceremoniously hoisted from the vault.

Suddenly, he laughed and got to his feet. "Sarge, could you get some of the lads in here? I just realised…the sarcophagus is facing the wrong way around. I'd like to turn it over if you don't mind, but it's too heavy for me on my own. I'd probably damage it further if I tried."

A few moments later, four burly policemen filed into the back office. They took hold of the coffin, more gently than when they had hauled it in, and turned it around as Jack instructed.

"I have a feeling this is going to be something special," Jack murmured, lighting a cigarette. "So we need to have a care, eh, lads?"

Once the coffin was face-forward, Jack got down beside it again. His knees creaked and gave out shocks of pain. "Not getting any younger," he grumbled, as he pulled on a plastic glove and passed his hand over the damaged surface. He ran a questing finger over one grime-caked area again and again. It felt *different* to the other metal.

"Sarge, have you got a soft cloth I could use for a moment?"

"Dish rag do?"

"Yes…but you'll have to throw it out after."

"I think we can manage without."

A damp crumpled cloth smelling of Fairy Liquid was thrust into Jack's hand. With gentle circular motions, he began to wipe the section that felt rough in comparison to the rest.

After a few minutes of cleaning, he gave an excited whoop. Dirt was crumbling away before the onslaught of the washing-up liquid on the dishrag, and he could see a plaque, like a little scroll, fastened to the lead surface. "I have something here, something important. I…I can see writing!"

Hand shaking a little, he reached into his pocket, drawing out the glasses he used for close-up work. He could see two words in a fancy script. On closer inspection, he realised it was Latin. One word said '*filia*'—daughter—and the other said '*Rex*'—king. This was no medieval nun, nor was it a child from a wealthy merchant family.

He shot upright, face flushed with excitement. "I was right. This is an important find. Quick, I need to get on the phone. We must get a specialist in medieval Latin out here before the twenty-four-hour deadline is up."

"Who do you think the coffin belonged to?" The Sargeant poked his head into the office.

"I'll be honest, I have no idea," said Jack Barnet. "But it's a young girl we have here…and I think she may be royal."

The translator, Clive Greaves, appeared first thing the next morning, a dry and dusty fellow with thinning yellowish hair and a face of similar hue, his eyes made enormous by the thick glass in his spectacles. Turning down an offer of a cuppa, he went right to work on the plaque attached to the coffin, cleaning every letter meticulously to reveal the wording. As he uncovered each new word, he quickly pencilled it down on a notepad.

When he was done, Greaves stood up and faced Jack Barnet and Sergeant Lords. He cleared his throat.

"Come on, don't keep us in suspense," said Jack. "Did you find out who she is?"

Greaves nodded and lifted up his notepad, deciphering his own spider-like scribbles. "The inscription reads, more or less, as follows: "*Here lies Anne, Duchess of York, daughter and heiress of John, late Duke of Norfolk, Earl Marshal, Earl of Nottingham and Warenne, Marshal of England, Lord of Mowbray, Segrave and Gower. Late wife of Richard Duke of York, second son of the most illustrious Prince Edward the Fourth, King of England and France, and Lord of Ireland, who died at Greenwich on the 19th day of November in the year of Our Lord 1481 and the 21st year of the said Lord King.*"

There was a moment of stunned silence. Jack spoke first. "Edward IV. That's the time of the Wars of the Roses"

"Correct," said Clive Greaves, with a sniff that made him sound like a schoolmaster surprised that his dullest student had answered a question correctly. "The child in the coffin was married to Edward IV's son, Richard."

The Sergeant, as he had already stated, was not a history lover; names and dates confused him. "Richard? I only know of one Richard from around that time…that hump-backed murderer in Shakespeare."

Clive Greaves peered down his long nose, his mouth pursing. "No, not, not *that* Richard—he was Edward IV's brother and probably not a 'hunchback' anyway; the Tudors almost certainly used some minor deformity as a means of propaganda, which was later taken up by that crass Shakespeare fellow."

"Not a fan of the Bard then." Jack folded his arms and grinned.

"No, a most overrated writer, in my opinion…that's if he even wrote those plays himself." Greaves cleared his throat. "But let's return to the matter at hand, shall we? The Richard mentioned on the plaque was Edward's younger son…and he was one of the infamous 'Princes in the Tower.'"

Sergeant Lords shook his head in amazement. "So you were right, Jack. Old royalty. We'd best call the Museum right away and see if they want to take a look…or better, take this coffin and its contents off our hands."

Jack nodded. "And, thank God, now we know who's inside, there's no way she'll be dumped in a public mass grave."

A van from the Museum arrived at the police station by mid-afternoon. News had spread throughout the surrounding area about the find at old St Trinity's and tongues were endlessly wagging—soon, it seemed, everyone in London was aware the sarcophagus was at the police station. And so, by the time the

Museum's van drew up, a large crowd had gathered outside the station doors, many of them press photographers.

"What can you tell us?" the press men shouted, as the coffin, draped in an old rug to foil the cameras, was carried out by several grave-faced Museum attendants and police. "Is it Roman? Medieval? Tudor?"

"We can tell you it's medieval," said Clive Greaves in a loud, clipped voice. "Now can you make way? This shouldn't become a grand spectacle."

"Surely you can tell us more! Is the body male or female?"

"The contents of the coffin have not been observed," replied Greaves. "But I can say this—it is close to one-hundred percent certain that they shall turn out, upon examination, to belong to a female."

One brisk young fellow in a trilby hat pushed to the fore of the scrum, scribbling down Clive Greaves' words on his notepad. "There must be some indication of the identity for you to be so certain of the sex," he said. "I am guessing by your statement she is identifiable in some way. Maybe...nobility, royalty? There was once a convent on the site of St Trinity's chapel, and several of notable women were interred there in the Middle Ages..."

Greaves' lips thinned and his eyes narrowed. "No comment."

"I've hit on it, haven't I?" the young journalist smirked. "Let's see...What's a good headline—*The Princess in the Police Station*?"

"No comment!" Clive Greaves barked again, and he climbed into the passenger seat of the Museum's van, while the Sergeant and his boys attempted to clear away the milling crowds, even surged in front of the van as it moved off.

By the next morning, the newspapers rolled off the presses and hit every news agent and corner stand in London—and across the country.

Written in bold, black typeface, the title '*The Princess in the Police Station*' leapt from every front page.

Archaeologists, anthropologists, bone specialists and others from the London Museum crowded into the dim little examining room in Guy's Hospital, where the coffin from the Minories had been brought. This was the big day…the sarcophagus would finally be opened and its contents revealed. Public interest was at a high; after the Museum's own specialists had confirmed the medieval date and the translation of the scroll plaque, an official press release had been sent out naming the burial as that of Anne Mowbray, child-bride of Prince Richard of Shrewsbury. The child's association with one of the 'Princes in the Tower' created a worldwide buzz.

"I wouldn't expect too much," said one of the researchers, pointing to two deep dents in the sarcophagus. "It's been punctured twice—see? One puncture at the neck, another at the foot. The coffin's not airtight."

"We'll see what we'll see," replied one of his colleagues, a bit more cheerfully, as he waved a blunt, broad knife. "I think this should do the trick. Lead is soft; the medieval soldering won't hold out for long. It should be almost as easy as opening a tin!"

An insertion was made, with the lead splitting easily as predicted. As the lid of the sarcophagus was carefully pried off, audible gasps came from all those gathered to observe, record and study.

Anne Mowbray's bones lay in disarray, jumbled by the act of dragging the coffin out of the burial crypt. Her pelvis was broken, her ribs scattered about like thin twigs; only her skull remained in its original position.

A skull which bore both the remnants of skin and scalp and masses and masses of vividly red hair. Hair that in Anne's lifetime, before it was stripped of melanin in the darkness of the grave, had been a shade of rich chestnut brown.

The Duke of Norfolk was furious when he read the news of Anne's discovery and that her coffin had been opened without so much as a 'by your leave'. He demanded that his distant relative be reburied at once, with all the honours due to her. Letters hit the papers, slamming 'modern disrespect towards the dead'—and how the body should have been left in situ until proper authorities could have excavated it.

"We probably don't have much time," muttered Dr John Limehouse, leader of the archaeological team—a tall man with thick, greying dark hair and heavy, scholarly black-framed glasses. "With all the bad press, I fear we are not going to be able to investigate the Minories body for very long. A once in a lifetime opportunity—to study the partly preserved body of a medieval noble—may well be lost."

One of the younger team members groaned. This was the most exciting archaeological program he had ever participated in. "It's madness. She's been dead for centuries! Do people always scream so loudly every time an old skeleton is evaluated?"

"Not normally, but it becomes trickier with a named individual…especially one once married to a member of the royal family. We'd better get a move on to do what we can before the axe falls."

Springtime arrived in London, bringing the first waves of milling tourists, the scent of petrichor on rainy days and the acrid odour of exhaust fumes. Several important assessments of Anne's burial and health before death were complete but no one knew if they would be able to proceed with more extensive testing.

What the archaeologists had found out was astounding.

After death, Anne's body had been wrapped in twelve layers of beeswax-coated cerecloth, which is what had aided the preservation of some of her tissue. Fungus and mould grew upon the cloth in livid grey and green blotches, almost obliterating the fine gold traceries woven into the shroud. Anne's hair was twisted and threaded with strips of the cerecloth, but her face was shrouded by a *sudarium,* a loose 'sweat-cloth'. A cushion lay beneath her head, decayed and fragmentary, once filled with sweet herbs that would have benefited those who came to see her body lying in state after her demise.

In life, the Duchess had stood only a few inches over four feet, much smaller than a child of almost nine in modern times—closer to the height of a six-year-old. Poor health was deduced by her atrophied hair roots, and the hair itself contained unusually high quantities of arsenic, which was often used as a medicine in medieval times. Her fingernails and toe nails were well preserved but had turned black with time. Still, they showed traces of being carefully manicured.

A press conference was held when these initial assessments were done, going over the pertinent finds of the archaeologists and pathologists. There was much talk of where Anne Mowbray should be reburied, with Westminster being the favoured location. The Dean had yet to confirm a space for her, however.

Almost immediately a hand shot up from among the gathered members of the press. "Question!"

Dr Limehouse gestured in the journalist's direction. "Yes?"

"I've been wondering all along... The body in the coffin is definitely Anne Mowbray, everything points to that, but why was she found in the ruins of a nunnery? I checked, and documents of the time said she was buried in St. Erasmus's chapel. The present Dean and Chapter of Westminster clearly thought she was still under the flagstones somewhere in the Abbey, otherwise they would not have given permission to open the coffin."

"Which they shouldn't have anyway," someone grumbled in the sea of coats, caps and cameras.

Dr Limehouse addressed the first journalist who had spoken. "You are correct, Anne Mowbray *was* buried in Westminster Abbey with all the respect due to a princess. However, as you may be aware, the Yorkist regime came to an end with the death of Richard III on Bosworth Field in 1485... Henry VII, who won the throne in battle, decided on Westminster Abbey to build his own grand chapel for the future burial of himself and his wife, Elizabeth of York. This rebuild meant the almost complete destruction of St. Erasmus' chapel and the original tomb of Anne Mowbray. There was no option for reinterment in the Abbey, so the nuns took in the remains. Why Henry acted so coldly towards this dead child, I cannot say. Perhaps the new King wanted few reminders of the former Yorkist reign—but, whatever his reason, Henry VII essentially threw young Anne Mowbray out of her grave."

A single chattering magpie, weak sun gleaming on its black and white plumage, flew over the ramparts of Framlingham Castle.

Elizabeth, Dowager Duchess of Norfolk, watched the bird soar towards the nearby deer park as she trailed listlessly along the wall walk along the battlements. Magpies…birds of ill repute, always prying and stealing.

One for sorrow, the villagers said.

Atop the wall, the sharp eastern wind cut her to the bone; even though winter had finally left England, it seemed its last vestiges clung to Suffolk, or, more specifically, to Elizabeth. Distracted, she rubbed her icy fingers; she had forgotten her gloves in her haste to leave the confines of her chambers where memories assailed her night and day. She did not care about the cold; the ache in her hands at least reminded her that she lived, that she had not turned to ice, her heart frozen and lifeless in her breast.

Less than two months ago, she was a happy woman. A babe grew within her belly, her second child in twenty years of marriage to John Mowbray, Duke of Norfolk. The awaited male heir the couple longed for and a playmate for their small daughter, Anne. Both children were conceived only after pilgrimages to the Shrine of Walsingham, where Richeldis, Lady of the Manor, once beheld the Virgin in a pool of golden light. At last, it felt as if her barren years were truly over, that she and John were favoured by God and Our Lady, and the Norfolk succession finally assured.

Elizabeth and John had wintered in Norwich, celebrating Christmas there in their ducal manor near the cathedral's Ethelbert Gate, in the area of town known as Tombland. The pregnancy had made Elizabeth unwell and the Mowbrays' physician and a local midwife said she must stay in Norwich, resting quietly, until the child was safely born. That was acceptable, if not ideal, since their daughter, whom they called Little Nan to differentiate from all the other Annes in their family, was at Framlingham with her nursemaids. But in no way would the Duke and Duchess jeopardise the possible arrival of a male heir.

In early January, however, John received news of poachers around Framlingham, and other spates of lawlessness in the local villages—a church robbed, a cleric beaten, livestock spirited off. Elizabeth remembered her husband's tender kiss upon her forehead before he took horse for Framlingham to deal with the trouble, and the words he had spoken as he put his foot into the stirrup: "Take care, dearest wife. I shan't be gone long. I will return to you when this problem is duly quelled and the miscreants brought to justice. I shall give your love to our little Nan and tell her you soon will be home with her new brother."

John reached Framlingham safely, according to reports…but within two days he was dead, suddenly and of no known cause. He went to dinner, laughed and jested with the household staff; by midnight his colour greyed and he fell to the floor like a stone. He was only one-and-thirty years old.

Throat tightening with grief, Elizabeth recalled the night the messengers arrived in Norwich. Snow was falling, the cathedral's spire a white needle prodding a flat, ominous sky. Torches made puddles of golden light on wave-like drifts in street and courtyard.

The couriers, dark-cloaked but bearing the Lion of Mowbray badges on the shoulder, told her the news without preamble. The shock was like a physical blow and she had collapsed on the doorstep. She made no sound but her loyal maid, Jane Rodon, had screamed and screamed. Members of the household leapt to assist; but there was blood on her skirts, too much blood.

By the dawn, the snowfall had ceased…and so had the life of her much-wanted infant, born blue and still. A boy, the much-wanted heir to the Dukedom of Norfolk.

Elizabeth took a shuddering breath. The chill air misted before her chapped, sore lips, bitten to the quick; her hand clutched the stones of the crenels for support. John was beyond all pain, but what was left for her, and even more important for her only child, her three-year-old daughter, Anne?

Anne, who would now inherit her father's vast wealth, who would be a great heiress and a valuable bride for some rapacious noble...

Shivers coursed down Elizabeth's slight frame at the thought of countless suitors, cruel young men with violent pasts, old men seeking renewed glory and gold. Every day was like this for her now. It was as if a dark cloud hung over her head, a shroud of doubt and gloom that, in the depth of the night, wound around her throat like strangling hands, so that she awoke panting for air, her hair in disarray and her hands trembling.

She wished her sister was here to comfort her, but Eleanor had lain in her grave in Norwich's House of the Carmelites for nigh on eight years. In life, Eleanor had suffered too—a love beyond imagining had turned to desertion and despair...and danger. Eleanor had gone from being a knight's widow to something else again, something dangerous not only to her but to those she loved. To those who knew her secret...

Elizabeth often wondered how Eleanor had died. She had been staying at Elizabeth's manor of Endhall at the time. Lonely but pious, travelling to Whitefriars frequently as a Carmelite *conversa*, she had recently given Elizabeth her property at Fenny Compton. "I have no need of it," she said, with that small sad smile Elizabeth was used to seeing. "I have no need of fleshly of earthly possessions anymore."

Elizabeth had then left England, attending upon Margaret of York at her marriage to Charles, Duke of Burgundy. When she returned, she found out her sister was dead. As with John, none knew what had killed the thirty-two-year-old Eleanor, who was interred in her beloved Whitefriars.

Shivering again, Elizabeth wrapped her furred mantle tightly about her before beginning the descent from Framlingham's walls. She must not dwell on all that had befallen, for little Nan's sake. She must be strong...but wary too.

Some years ago, the same year Eleanor had died so unexpectedly two trusted servants of her household, John Poynings and Richard Alford, accused of treason by the King for supposedly engaging in a Lancastrian plot. Found guilty in a swift trial, they were hanged, drawn and quartered—a most dreadful death.

Elizabeth was dubious about their guilt, however; to the best of her knowledge, her household was unswervingly loyal to the crown. She wondered if her servants' executions were a warning to her—a warning to keep silent about what she knew about her sister and Edward.

The secret that could cause his kingship to crumble…The secret of his clandestine marriage to Eleanor, a union abandoned by the womanising King but never legally dissolved. The marriage that by laws of God and Man made Edward Plantagenet a bigamist and his children bastards.

Elizabeth entered the castle, mounting the staircase to the apartments and hurrying along the dim corridors to the nursery. Reaching it, she found Little Nan awake, her nurses looking on smilingly as the little girl tried to comb the hair of a poppet with her fingers. The poppet was one John had once brought for her in Norwich; ragged with use, its knotted dyed red hair and bone-white face gave it an almost ghoulish aspect. Elizabeth hated it but Nan clung to the doll, and as it was a gift from the child's father, and now there would be no other, it would stay.

As Elizabeth approached and the nursemaids bobbed curtseys, little Nan glanced up from her ministrations on her poppet. Her eyes were brown like her mother's, an inheritance from her grandfather, the great warrior John Talbot, Earl of Shrewsbury, but her chestnut hair, thick and waving even at her young age, was the image of her father's.

"Mama?" Nan dropped her doll to the floor. It lay there, limbs sprawled, like a miniature dead body. "Papa?"

Nan was too young to understand what had happened to her father, the Duke, or that she would never see him again in this life. Nor did she know that by dying so unexpectedly, John Mowbray had left her both rich and extremely vulnerable.

"No, your papa is not here, Nan." Elizabeth ruffled her daughter's hair. Curls slid like precious swatches of silk between her fingers. "But I will take you to the chapel where you may say a prayer for his sweet soul. You remember how to do that, don't you, my sweetling? Go down on your knees and ask gentle Jesus to look after your father?"

Nan nodded solemnly, but looked a little dismayed; her lower began to tremble. She missed her papa's presence. Why was he not here to dandle her on his knee and let her frolic with his dogs?

Apprehensive, Elizabeth bit her lip, drawing a bead of blood. What a poor mother she was; she had upset her own poor child. "Do not cry. Maybe we shall do prayers together later, Nan…but for now, come with me to the garden. Your cheeks are paler than they should be. You need fresh air. Too many evil humours gather inside a castle in the winter months."

The gardens of Framlingham Castle were one of the castle's latest and most distinctive features, but they were bleak now, the ground frozen solid and the rosebushes naked and thorny as they twined through skeletal trellises. The berry bushes still bore red fruitsN though, and the rosehips were fat to bursting, ready to be plucked by the cook's apprentices to make into sweet jelly.

Little Nan was wrapped in a heavy cloak and towing along her ragged poppet. Coming to the edge of the shallow fish pond, covered by a wafer-thin sheet of ice, she put out her foot to touch the glittering crust.

Elizabeth grabbed her under the arms and swept her away, trembling. "No, you must never do that, Anne. There is water under the ice; it is deep and it is dangerous."

Anne's eyes widened then began to spill slow, fat tears. She stared down at her feet, ashamed by her mother's chastisement.

Elizabeth's lady-in-waiting, Jane Rodon, who was trundling behind her mistress and her small daughter, intervened to save the day and stave off the child's tears. "Look, Lady Anne, I have brought something for you. A little gift!"

She held out a circlet wrought of thin silver wires and ivy vines, with each pointed tine decorated by a blood-red haw stolen from the nearby bushes. "I found this out in the deer park," she said, casting a knowing look to the dowager duchess. "To be so finely garlanded, I am sure it once belonged to the Queen of the Faeries herself. Now, Anne, it is forever yours."

The child reached up, taking the circlet and setting it atop her head. "I am now a faery princess," she chattered, twirling around the edge of the pond, her prior tears forgotten. "A real princess!"

A cloud-shadow darted across the sun and the wintry light dipped and became cold blue. A rush of primordial fear gripped Elizabeth's heart. As a child, her nursemaids, a gaggle of plain-spoken country women, had told her it was unlucky to tempt the Queen of Faerie—but she was grown now and knew such tales were superstitious twaddle. No such creature existed save in the minds of the superstitious and she was a pious Christian woman.

And yet…

"Anne, you had best take that garland off before it snarls your hair," she muttered, ignoring her daughter's crestfallen face and the hurt and embarrassment in Jane's eyes.

Little Nan snatched the circlet and flung it on the ground with an uncharacteristic burst of temper before bursting into noisy sobs. The red haws broke loose and rolled like tiny severed heads across the ground.

A rider was at the gate; Elizabeth heard the rattle of his horse's hooves on the ice-slick woodwork of the drawbridge. It was early, she had not long risen and heard Mass; she was expecting no one. Perhaps the newcomer was some kinsman or a kindly soul from afar sending condolences for John's death.

But, somehow, she knew that was not the case. She had dreamed the last few nights, of something great and terrible that would engulf her and her daughter. For herself she cared little, now that John was dead, but Little Nan—such a tiny, fragile leaf to be blown about in the face of an incoming storm.

A rustle of fabric sounded in the hallway leading to the solar; Elizabeth glanced up as her steward entered the chamber and bowed. "Your Grace, a messenger waits without. Shall I grant admission?"

"Does he seem of good intent? Is his quest urgent? I have little time for visitors unless their mission is of great importance; I am still in mourning." She gestured to her black velvet robes, their sombreness alleviated only by the silver rosary threaded through her girdle.

The steward wrang his hands, his brow creased with worry. "I fear it is *very* important, your Grace. He wears the King's livery."

Elizabeth paled; Jane, sitting in the window seat behind, reached out to steady her. "I can hardly turn a messenger from King Edward, can I?" she said, with a wan, bitter smile. "Send him to me, James."

The steward bowed again and hastened from the solar. Elizabeth waited in silence. Despite the heat from the fire glowing in the fireplace, a cold chill, a frisson of dread, skewered her to the marrow. So many times lately she had felt that chill, as if the hand of Death himself reached out to touch her, taunt her.

But it was not Death she feared. Her conscience was clean and surely heaven would await if she should depart the mortal life still young.

What truly made her blood run cold was human, but held power over her from which she could never truly escape.

The King.

All women loved Edward, it was said—the handsomest prince in Europe, tall as a tower, deep-voiced, and with the courage of a lion.

Elizabeth was the exception

She feared Edward, Fourth of that Name, the victor of Towton, Barnet and Tewkesbury, more than anything else in the world—not so much for herself but for her household and for her daughter. She could not forget her executed servants or the two pardons given to her and her brother Humphrey Talbot—pardons for supposed sins while in Burgundy with Duchess Margaret's entourage that neither truly understood. In retrospect, she believed the mysterious pardons were intended as another dire warning. *I already have my eyes on you, Eleanor Talbot's kin...*

She raised her bowed head as a figure filled the solar's arched doorway. Shadows stretched towards her, dark and threatening. A Sunne in Splendour badge blazed on the man's shoulder, light in the darkness, but it was not a cheerful light but one that might burn her very soul to ashes.

"Enter!" she said sternly, trying to impress her authority as the Dowager Duchess of Norfolk. She dared show no weakness, yet neither must she cause gross offence to Edward's man.

The King's messenger strode in, casting back his cloak with a flourish and revealing a tabard with the royal arms flashing blue and gold. She almost laughed at his flouncing, grandiose gesture; what a popinjay! She schooled herself to keep a grave countenance.

The messenger sidled up to her seat, a haughty-looking young man with finely cut and curled hair. His bow was curt, perfunctory, as he handed Elizabeth a sealed letter. "His Grace, King Edward, has told me to remain at Framlingham until you give your answer," he said, his tones clipped and blunt.

Elizabeth's eyes blurred and her head felt light. If the letter held what she feared, there was only one answer she could give. It was not the answer she *wanted* to give, but who dared say 'no' to a King, especially a King like Edward Plantagenet.

Read it, Elizabeth, you must not lose face, must not appear feeble... She fumbled with the letter, the wax cracking and falling in pieces on her lap, the image of the mounted ruler with his shield of lilies and leopards breaking apart, his upraised sword harmlessly brushing her fingertips.

In silence, she let her gaze travel down the words written on the parchment. She froze, breath catching in her throat. She could feel eyes boring into her; the arrogant messenger's and those of Jane and her other two ladies. A terrible silence descended over the room—it stretched on and on, long and uncomfortable. Elizabeth heard the shuffle of the messenger's booted feet, impatient, irritated.

Let him wait. He is nothing to you…

Elizabeth quickly regained her equilibrium once the King's written words were digested. She wrapped herself in a cloak of chill hauteur, masking her true feelings—hiding that she wanted to shout and scream and drive this hateful minion of Edward from her home. *I am like a mummer*, she thought, as she stood slowly, the rustle of her skirt the only sound in the solar.

"You may depart back to London, messenger," she said. "Tell the King I am always loyal and always his to command. His will shall be done, although there must still be further negotiations about irregularities in …*this*."

She lifted King Edward's letter, shaking it slightly…or was it just that her hand shook? She hoped her pose was a little disrespectful, not enough to invoke anger, but enough to show she was not completely cowed by the contents of the King's missive.

The messenger's mouth grew sour, giving him a petulant look. "I will bear your message to his Grace, Dowager," he said curtly, "if I have your leave to depart. The King is eager for an answer."

"You may depart at once, sir," she said, with an unfriendly smile. "The sooner the better."

The youth left, his footsteps clattering in the hall as the steward ushered him out to the courtyard and his waiting mount.

"My Lady?" Jane was instantly at her side. "Are you well? Is all well?"

Elizabeth took a deep breath. "No…I am not well, Jane. The King…the King wants what I feared most."

Jane's forehead creased with worry. Elizabeth turned to gaze into her loyal companion's face. She knew her maid feared that Edward had 'seen' Lancastrian plots among Elizabeth's servants again, putting the entire household into disrepute and maybe even bringing about disgrace and death, as happened before.

Jane was wrong. This blow was to Elizabeth alone…and to Anne. Dear little Nan, so young, her father so recently buried.

Shameful tears began to well. It was not seemly to weep in front of one's staff, who were meant to look up to a highborn lady as a model of propriety and strength. But the flow would not stop, the dam was breached.

Elizabeth pressed her hands over her face as she cried, "Oh, Jane, the worst possible thing has happened. King Edward has purchased Anne's wardship—and he also wants her to marry his second son, Richard of Shrewsbury!"

Elizabeth sat primly in the back of the chariot as it rumbled along the rutted roads towards London. Little Nan, now aged five, was seated between her nurses and Jane Rodon, peeking shyly at her mother, who had been silent and downcast for most of the journey. The little girl was dressed in a yellow silk gown embroidered with white roses for her royal husband's family and several small Norfolk lions to represent her own. Her luxuriant auburn hair curled about her cheeks, overwhelming her elfin features but creating a frame for her large brown eyes.

"Why do you look so sad, mama?" Anne asked after a while. "I am getting married. I shall be a great princess! Is that not good, mama?"

"Of course it is good, my darling." Elizabeth prayed that she sounded convincing. *It will be more like a funeral than a wedding,* she thought bitterly, glancing outside the curtain on the chariot's window at the frozen countryside drifting by. *Even the land is dead, blighted by winter. Edward could not even wait till spring for the wedding, so eager he is to make certain his younger son has his future assured.*

The marriage contract had been agreed upon, after some half-hearted wrangling on Elizabeth's behalf, which she knew would come to nought, not with the King's multitude of shrewd, rapacious lawyers. As she had guessed from the start, Elizabeth ended up with little benefit from the union, other than the prestige of having a daughter married to a prince and whatever that might bring. She had relinquished a large portion of her jointure and dower lands in favour of Nan and Richard. That was bad enough, but there was worse in the contract than that. Edward had pushed for a special act that gave his son full claim on all the lands and titles of Norfolk should Anne die before her husband without giving him an heir. That meant the cousins and other kin of her husband John would be excluded, if the worst happened, from what they saw as their rightful inheritance.

Elizabeth scowled, her mood as dark as the day. The act was horrible, utterly horrible—it almost assumed that Anne *would* die young and childless, or at least that is how it read to Elizabeth. Yet what could she have done to make it any different? Refusal to accept would have been…*unwise*…and so many depended on her to keep them from harm: her Talbot family, her Norfolk household.

She thought about the recent news about the King's brother, George of Clarence. The man had seemingly gone mad when his wife, Elizabeth's cousin Isabel, and newborn child had died, raving of poison and blaming the Duchess' servants and even the Sheriff of Wiltshire, who was once his friend. He had pursued his wife's lady, Ankaret Twynyho, into the far west of England, dragging the elderly woman all the way to Warwick, where he had her hanged after a sham trial. Not content with murder, he then sought a necromancer, Thomas Burdett, who imagined Edward's demise—an act punishable by death—and made rhymes claiming that his son, Prince Edward, would never reign. When a drunken George finally burst into a council session, shouting that Edward himself was a sorcerer who cast spells on his subjects, it was too much for the King. His brother was arrested and hauled to the Tower, where he dwelt now, his ultimate fate still uncertain.

No, if King Edward showed no leniency to those who crossed him, even members of his own family, he would certainly not show it to the sister of Eleanor Talbot. What she knew was perilous to so many… She must remain discreet, quiet, and pliant, putting no foot wrong. For little Nan's sake above all.

Harsh laughter grated in her throat; she choked it back, feigning a cough, not wanting her daughter to hear. To Elizabeth, it felt as if Anne was going to become a hostage for her mother's good behaviour as much as she was going to become a bride. And if anything should happen to Nan, all would become Richard of Shrewsbury's, setting him up to live in the splendour a royal duke should exhibit. He would possess the Norfolk inheritance and be free to marry a foreign princess to add to his riches…

Up ahead, through the chariot's window, Elizabeth caught a glint of sun on ice; of light dancing on slow, turgid water where passing boats had broken through the drifting floes. She guessed it was the Thames, partly frozen in the bitterly cold weather of the past week. Even as she watched, shrieking peasant children with bone skates lashed to their ankles skidded out across the ice, intent on play. She cringed, fearful the frozen surface might shatter like a mirror and send them to their deaths, and then acerbic mirth rose in her throat again, tart as bile—she too was skating on thin ice, wondering which way to move for safety.

"Where are we, mama?" Nan was licking a piece of barley sugar given to her by one of the nursemaids. "We have been in here for so long. My toes are cold."

"Ellen." Elizabeth nodded at the nursemaid, who shifted her bulk off her cushion and leaned down to wrap a fur around Nan's dainty little feet. They both had started the day with newly-heated stones in their shoes, but after so many hours the warmth had faded.

"We have almost reached London, my dearest," she then told her daughter. She took Nan's hand; although gloved, she could feel the coldness of the little girl's fingers even through the rabbit skin. She rubbed them gently, lovingly. Anne was not the most robust of children. Every winter, she suffered coughs and wheezing, and her appetite was often poor. If anything should befall her, once she was out of Elizabeth's care…

"I wonder if Richard will like me," Nan suddenly blurted. "He is younger than me, so maybe he won't."

"I am sure he will, Anne. He is well brought up as a King's son. He may not quite understand the solemnity of marriage at his young age, but he will learn in time. Why, you will grow up together, and with any luck, you will become friends and playmates—and that will set you on course for a happy future life together."

Nan looked unconvinced and a little tearful. "Maybe. But mama, why can I not stay with you till Richard and I reach the proper age for *real* married people? I will miss you so much."

Elizabeth tried to radiate confidence even as her own eyes grew wet. She stared over her daughter's head, endeavouring to hide her sorrow. "The King has made you his ward, my sweeting. You are to live with Queen Elizabeth in her household until you are of an age to abide with Richard. Other little girls live there: the Princesses Elizabeth, Cecily, and Mary. I am sure they will prove themselves boon companions and help your adjustment into royal life."

"II thought I wanted to be a princess once, mama," Anne whispered, "but now…I am scared. I wish I was back at Framlingham."

"I know, Nan, but one day you will laugh at your fears. You will be happy…"

"Are *you* happy?"

Her little daughter's expected question made her cheeks burn. *From the mouths of innocent babes…*

"Yes, my sweet Nan, of course I am happy," she said, her smile frozen on her lips and her eyes still averted from the child's wide, forthright stare. "Never happier. We are so honoured, Anne. Never forget that. Honoured."

The carriage rolled on towards the immense city of London. The road teemed with people now, wool-clad peasants and tradesmen, nuns in covered chariots painted with holy symbols, monks with frozen bare toes riding on ill-tempered asses, journeymen with satchels strapped to their backs, weary pilgrims sporting multiple badges from their travels, merchants on horseback dressed in furred cloaks, traders bringing in goods for the marketplace or to sell to London's numerous shopkeepers.

Elizabeth glanced out the chariot window into the falling dusk. Frost speckled the verges of the road; the rest was a sea of churned mud, clogging the wheel-spokes and slowing the progress of her carriage. In the distance, through foggy murk, she caught a glimpse of London's wall—high, adamant, standing on Roman foundations—and behind them the tops of tiered houses and church spires.

She was glad the long, uncomfortable journey was almost over, but there would be no relaxation for either her or Anne. The carriage was taking her, not to the Norfolk townhouse, but straight to Westminster Palace, where the King and Queen would greet her and their future daughter-in-law. It was not the first time Elizabeth had met the royal family, of course; she had visited court many times when John was alive and had known Margaret of York well enough to accompany her on her journey to Burgundy. But it was the first time since John's death, and she had always felt her husband had stood as a shield, if only a fragile one, between her and the King, although she had never told him of the betrayal of her sister and the danger it brought to all their lives.

She glanced over at Anne. Weary from the journey, the little girl had fallen asleep with her head cushioned in a nursemaid's broad lap. Let her rest; there would be little enough time for slumber later on, with all the good and great arriving for the wedding and all the formalities and ceremonies taking place.

With wheels creaking, the chariot rocked to an abrupt halt. The entourage had reached one of London's gates, a stern, heavy tower of mottled grey stone with crenelations fanged along its summit. Elizabeth was irritated by the delay, believing the party would have gained immediate entrance. After all, it was clear who they were. The cover of the chariot was painted with the arms of Mowbray impaled by the Arms of England. Yet, here they were stuck, waiting for approval, while vagrants and villeins poured under the gate arch, gawping and pointing. Some veered a bit too close, striving to get a look through the velvet curtain draping the window. Elizabeth wished she had something to throw, to drive them off. Her small band of guardsmen did their best, but they were sorely outnumbered by the swell of curious Londoners.

Suddenly, a trumpet wailed tinnily, its off-key notes offending the Dowager Duchess' ears. Poor little Nan stirred, frowning and mumbling in her sleep.

A shout went up amidst the crowd surrounding the chariot. "Make way for the Mayor!"

Ignoring the gapers still milling about the gate, Elizabeth peered through the fogged horn pane covering the chariot's window. The Mayor of London was emerging from the pedestrian entrance, in his billowing robes as red as blood with the aldermen in their violet garb filing respectfully behind him. Elizabeth's heart sank. She had no wish for long, drawn-out ceremonies, not here.

Her gaze was dragged upwards, past the stout form of the Mayor, to the top of the gateway, where a row of tarred traitors' heads grinned down, black and shrivelled, the teeth gleaming white against desiccated lips. Although the weather was bitterly cold, she imagined she could smell the sickly-sweet aroma of decay.

Anne was waking up, her mouth drawn in a yawn.

"Your Grace?" Elizabeth's Master of Horse appeared, trudging up to the chariot window. "The Mayor is here."

"Yes, I heard that," said Elizabeth waspishly. "What is his intention? I expected to be taken to Westminster without delay and without being ogled by oafs."

The man reddened, looking abashed. "He and his fellows are calling for Lady Anne—the 'High and Mighty Princess Anne', I should say. Perhaps just a glimpse will satisfy, my Lady…"

Elizabeth made an annoyed sound but nodded at the man. "Let the Mayor know her appearance will be brief, that the Princess must not risk her health by standing in the cold, breathing in the unpleasant humours of this city."

The man bowed and hastily fled away. "Nan, my dear." Elizabeth put her hand on her daughter's flushed cheek. "We have arrived in London. Many dignitaries have come to see you and escort our party to the palace."

"Is—is the King here…and Richard?" Anne's eyelids flickered, and she sat up, groggy from sleep, her hair flattened against her skull where she had lain on the nurse's lap.

A babe, not a princess, Elizabeth thought grimly, watching her.

"No, dear heart, it is the Mayor of London and the aldermen come to greet you. This will happen wherever you go from now on."

Elizabeth ruffled Nan's unruly locks with her fingers, making her look more presentable for the Mayor and other onlookers. She noticed how tired the child looked, blue circles ringing her eyes, her face lacking in colour save for the feverish flush high on her cheeks. "Do not fear. It will only be for a few minutes, Anne, and then we can continue on to Westminster."

Elizabeth stepped out of the chariot, aided by a waiting footman. More trumpets sounded a fanfare as Anne followed her, accompanied by Jane. The crowd stared, pushing forward; leathery faced street hawkers grinned, monks began praying loudly, stout dames in vast headdresses wide as gables commented loudly on every aspect of Anne's appearance, while scruffy rag-clad urchins ran about shrieking with excitement (and cutting off a few scrips from the belts of the unwary onlookers).

Anne turned in the direction of the Mayor, who towered over her like a huge red giant. "Welcome, O High and Mighty Princess!" he boomed as he made a huge, ostentatious bow, whipping off his velvet hat and bending so low his wispy grey beard almost swept the befouled cobblestones.

Little Nan stood in front of him, hands clasped nervously. She had been taught as well as a child her age could be, and in a tiny, trembling voice, she began, "Thank you for your greetings, I…"

She halted, frozen, words dying on her lips. She was staring upwards in shocked horror. Up at the grisly rows of severed heads that decorated the top of the gate, their eyes gone, the ever-present carrion birds trying to worry off morsels of tarred flesh.

Elizabeth stepped towards the traumatised child, and Nan, stumbling back from the Mayor, vomited all over the cobbles. The crowd gasped as if this had been a great *faux pas* and retreated, stumbling all over each other, perhaps fearing the child had some dire contagion.

"The Lady Anne has travelled long, and her digestion is unsettled by the ride," said Elizabeth hastily, her expression stern as if daring anyone to argue. The Mayor, his mouth open in a round 'O' of surprise, began to nod like a fool, clutching his hat against his burly chest.

"I understand, your Grace, fully understand." He whirled about, arms milling at the violet-robed aldermen. "Out of the way! Out of the way, I say. The Princess must pass through at once with no further ado."

Jane and the nursemaid called Ellen scooped up Anne and bore her back to the chariot, Elizabeth close behind, trying to shield her daughter's wide, terrified eyes from any more glimpses of the bird-pecked skulls spiked upon the gatehouse roof.

Once she was in the safety of the carriage and the wheels juddered forward, Elizabeth breathed a sigh of relief. Nan had thrown herself onto a tasselled pillow and was weeping silently.

Elizabeth had no idea how to console her. As the carriage proceeded into the streets beyond the gate, Anne finally glanced up, her eyes red, nose running. "I want to go home, mama. Please! I don't like it here. Tell the King I cannot marry Richard…"

"Nan, oh my sweet Nan…" Elizabeth felt her heart wrench at her daughter's overt distress. "All will be well. God will look after you, I promise. You must do your duty—to me, to your King, and to your father's memory. Your papa would want you to carry his bloodline into the royal family. Think of it, Nan, your children shall be royalty—what a great honour!"

Anne still stared blearily at her, teardrops quivering on her long lashes. An event so far in the future scarcely seemed real and brought no comfort. "But it…it's horrible here. I thought London would be magic, mama! A magic city! But dead heads were on the gate!"

"They were felons and traitors, Anne." Elizabeth grew solemn. "Wicked men who deserved to die."

But as the carriage trundled on over the cobblestones, she thought about her servants, executed for treason just after she arrived home from Burgundy all those years ago. Were they truly wicked? *Had* they truly deserved their fate?

The daylight outside the carriage suddenly dimmed. A great black cloud had rolled over London, and rain began to sluice down, beating upon the canvas roof of the chariot like a stream of frigid tears.

By the time Elizabeth and Anne arrived at Westminster, the downpour had grown even heavier. The chariot's covering had sprung an unexpected leak along the route, and both mother and daughter, teeth chattering and wrapped in sopping wet cloaks, were escorted to their quarters by the King's servants. Elizabeth had Jane and her other ladies dress her, while the fire braziers were stoked high, adding warmth to the chamber and making shadows dance across the tapestries adorning the walls.

"Bring bath water for the Lady Anne Mowbray," Elizabeth ordered as a servant appeared in the doorway, asking if anything further was required. "She is cold and must be warmed up and made comfortable."

The man looked uneasy but dared not argue. Bowing, he hurried from the room, his feet pattering on the stone stairs outside. Shortly thereafter, another visitor arrived—Elizabeth recognised the Lord Chamberlain, William Hastings, Edward's right-hand man and dearest friend, despite the large gap in their ages. Edward and William drank together, diced together, hunted together...and whored together, occasionally passing their paramours between them and to others within their circle. Or so the rumours said.

Will Hastings cleared his throat. "Greetings, Dowager Duchess. I am glad you and the Lady Anne arrived safely. The King and Queen are eager to see you both."

"I am sure," said Elizabeth, eyeing him. She thought his gaze lingered a fraction too long on her bosom. "However, Anne is but a child, and she is cold and weary from such a long journey. I have ordered bath water to be brought; I assume it will take a little time for the water to be boiled and brought up here."

Will Hastings licked his lips. "I understand your need for home comforts, your Grace, but the King is very impatient to see his future daughter-in-law, as you might imagine."

Elizabeth stepped closer to the Lord Chamberlain; she thought his eyes lit up a little at her proximity and she forced back the urge to break into mocking laughter. Well she knew that Hastings had aided the King in the secret marriage with her poor, gullible sister. Just as if she would ever bestow favours of any sort, let alone carnal ones, on such a man.

"My Lord Hastings," she said, forcing her lips into a pleasant smile. "My daughter is bedraggled and freezing. She is in no fit state to be presented to the royal family. If King Edward inquires again, tell him I will bring her to him in due time, when she has bathed, rested and been properly attired."

Hastings spluttered, his wind-leathered cheeks reddening. "B-but Dowager, you cannot…"

"I can, Will Hastings, and I will. Go to His Highness and if he asks where Anne is, tell him, from me—he will just have to wait."

Anne was dressed in scarlet velvet, a pearl circlet holding back her hair. She was less tearful now, having consumed a decent meal of stuffed eggs, cheese, beef tarts, and shrimp bathed in vinegar, but her little face was still pinched and filled with worry.

"It is time to go, Nan." Elizabeth extended a hand to her young daughter. "The King and Queen are waiting and have been for some time. We must keep them waiting no longer."

She cast a glance towards Will Hastings, who had returned to ask about their progress. He stood in the arched doorway, shuffling uncomfortably from foot to foot in his expensive poulaines. His mouth, normally fixed in a grin that some might call 'lascivious' was downturned. The King must not have been pleased when his friend returned without his future daughter-in-law.

Resigned, Anne nodded and let her mother lead her from the room. Hastings strutted along before them both, the keys of his office jingling on his jewelled belt, his thinning brown hair blowing out from his long forehead as he increased his speed.

The King must be very annoyed, thought Elizabeth, fighting back a smirk, despite herself. Hastings might be his closest friend and companion in debauchery, but she suspected that if Edward told him to jump, Baron Hastings would reply, 'How high, your Grace?'

Hastings soon brought Elizabeth and Nan to the King's room, a reception hall sometimes known as the 'Painted Chamber', which stood alongside the decorated chapel where, in two days, little Anne would marry young Prince Richard.

Taking a deep breath as Hastings announced her, Elizabeth swept into the chamber with Anne at her side, breathing heavily, like a rabbit facing a predator.

The hall was spectacular but overwhelming, meant to impress newcomers and foreign dignities alike. Vivid paintings covered the walls from top to bottom—the Virtues and Vices, biblical prophets and patriarchs, seraphim and cherubim, the battles of the Maccabees, Saint John wearing pilgrim's robes, and the Confessor himself at his own canonisation. Two lions roared at each other, equally fierce, and oddly out of place amidst the classic Biblical scenes.

Elizabeth's gaze was drawn to the chilling depiction of King Antiachus, enraged and malevolent as he leaned forward on his throne to pass sentence on death on a poor mother and her seven sons, who had defied him over their beliefs. The mother, arrayed in a pink gown and wearing a long veil, gazed proudly at her last living sons, one already under the torturer's knife while the other, clad in almost-royal purple with his hands bound, awaited death beside a blazing cauldron that held the limbs of the rest of her sacrificed children.

Elizabeth shuddered. Edward was no Antiachus, but, like that ancient monarch, he would not be crossed. Anne was *her* sacrifice; Edward wanted her daughter's blood, though not, of course, literally. The blood of Mowbray and Talbot would mingle with that of the Royal House, forming a pact, a sacred bond—one that required secrecy from Elizabeth for as long as she should live.

She shivered again and tore her gaze from the grim painting, fixing her eyes on the state bed at the far end of the long, narrow chamber. It was a noble structure, arrayed with silks and velvets in deep red and forest-green. Lions and Lilies in gold thread cascaded down its curtains, and its posts were painted with golden stars. A portrait of Edward the Confessor overlooked the bed—a replacement for a painting made in Henry III's time, which had been lost in a fire.

King Edward and Queen Elizabeth were sitting in ornamental chairs before the state bed, a blue silk canopy decorated with stars that mirrored the chamber's ceiling drawn over them. Servants and attendants clustered around them, making sure anything they wished for would be hastily obtained—young pages in silvered doublets, men wearing the Sunne in Splendour badge and the Rose en Soleil, ladies-in-waiting in silver tissue and samite—gorgeous, but not in such a way they might outshine the Queen.

The King was handsome, as Elizabeth remembered him, but not as breathtaking as when he was a young man of eighteen—around the time when her sister had fallen deeply, foolishly for him. The hard form of a peerless warrior had disappeared once he had begun his life of opulence; rolls of excess flesh pushed against the velvet of his fine purple and black doublet, and extra fleshiness softened the contours of his jaw and chin, dissolving its once square outline. No grey showed in his shoulder-length brown hair, though, and his hazel eyes were still bright and shrewd.

Elizabeth Woodville was, as ever, of exceptional beauty, just as her mother, Jacquetta of Luxembourg, had been in her youth. Tall and slender, showing little sign that she had borne numerous children, she wore a rose-hued gown trimmed with fur and decorated with seed pearls. Her headdress was huge, like silken sails, pulled back to reveal her high, milk-pale forehead and a few sleek strands of pale, moon-gold hair. Her eyelids were heavy and painted to emphasise her eyes, which were a deep green, their hue striking enough to be visible even at a distance. An air of bored hauteur clung to her, and her ladies were fussing around her in silence.

Elizabeth walked up to the King and Queen and made a deep curtsey. Anne followed beside her, so scared that she nearly fell while clutching her skirts in her clenched hands. Elizabeth noticed the corner of the Queen's lip quirk mockingly, or so it seemed, and anger flared within her, causing her ears and cheeks to burn. How dare she, queen or no!

Edward leaned forward, smiling at little Nan. At least, Elizabeth thought, his smile appeared quite genuine. "My greetings to you, my little daughter-to-be," he said. "You have nought to fear here. You will soon grow accustomed to the ways of the court. My dearest wife, the Queen, shall take you into her household and care for you as if you were her own—and, indeed, once the wedding has taken place, you shall forever be one of us."

"Thank you, your Grace!" Anne's voice was a high-pitched whisper.

Elizabeth noticed the Queen's lips purse, and then her cat-green eyes glazed over as if absolute boredom had overwhelmed her. She looked straight through Anne as her ladies-in-waiting fluttered some more, fanning her and refilling her cup.

"Your arrival was later than I expected, Dowager Duchess." Edward focused his attention on Elizabeth. His bright eyes had cooled, darkened; his mouth drew into a thin line. "I have waited long and put aside my own pursuits because of it. The Queen and I became quite concerned that you and the Lady Anne had been accosted on the road. We even wondered…" he let out a bellow of laughter that rang throughout the Painted Chamber, "if you'd maybe taken ship for the continent with our son's intended bride in tow!"

"No, your Grace, I would have never countenanced such a faithless act!" Elizabeth, was appalled that Edward thought she might flee even though she had agreed to the marriage contract. *He* was the faithless one, not her; she always kept her promises, even if they broke her heart in two. The promise to keep her sister's secret. The promise of daughter's hand-in-marriage, to protect both child and mother or so she hoped.

"I was merely jesting with you, Elizabeth," said the King, his demeanour growing warmer again. He slapped his thigh in mirth.

Elizabeth recoiled, stunned by his abrupt change in mood, his sudden familiarity. Next to him, the Queen narrowed her eyes and cast her husband a cold look. She then glanced over Anne as if remembering she was there, and then to Elizabeth with what? Distrust? Jealousy?

Sweat gathered at the nape of Elizabeth's neck, below the veil that streamed from her tall hennin. She was not here to make enemies, and she certainly had no designs on the King or indeed any other man. In her youth, when she had accompanied Lady Margaret to her wedding in Burgundy, she had been beautiful—minstrels had serenaded her and courtiers had spoken within her hearing of the 'beautiful English lady.' But that was in the past—care and grief had surely aged her, robbing her of her vaunted comeliness.

Edward had returned to a serious demeanour while the Queen went back to icy indifference. "Go now," said Edward. "It is best to get the child abed. The festivities will be long and tiring over the next few days."

Elizabeth curtseyed to the Yorkist King and his consort. "As you wish, your Grace."

She beckoned to Anne to likewise curtsey, which she did with greater skill than the first time, but even as the girl rose, she glanced at her mother with a furrowed brow. "Mama," she said, her voice coming out surprisingly loud in that vast room, "where is Prince Richard? Will I not meet my husband today?"

It was the Queen's turn to laugh, but Elizabeth cringed at the sound, which was frosty, almost mocking. Nonetheless, she alighted from her seat, a shimmering vision in rose, almost like a mythic queen—or a sorceress—in some heroic tale of old, and placed her long, smooth hands on either side of little Nan's face. Anne blinked up at her, overawed and fighting back terror.

"Oh, my dearest little child." Elizabeth Woodville's voice was like frozen honey. "Richard is abed as befits a child his age. He is younger than you, remember. It hardly matters if you meet before the wedding; he is a typical boy, ready to play with pups and worms, and has no truck with little maids, not even his sisters. There is no need for you to have a formal introduction, for married you shall be whether you know or like each other or not."

The Queen then returned to her seat, leaving Anne standing in embarrassment and dismay.

Casting a slightly rueful look at his acid-tongued Queen, Edward made another motion at Elizabeth and Anne. "Go, and a good night to you, Dowager Duchess."

Elizabeth hurried towards the door leading from the Painted Chamber to the apartments, Anne clutching her hand in a tight, sweaty grip.

As she neared the doorway, the Dowager Duchess noticed the words written in French above the arch: '*He who has and does not give, will not receive.*'

She bit her lip till she tasted the iron tang of blood. She had given all that was the best of her to Edward and his family—but she feared with all her heart what she would receive in turn.

Elizabeth woke early, her breath labouring in her lungs and a sense of panic rising in her chest. Was she ill? She could not be, must not be, on this day of all days!

Gradually, as light began to creep under the wooden window shutters and Jane rose to throw some kindling into the brazier, the horrible sensations passed, and she climbed stiffly from her bed, groaning as if she were an old woman, onto the soft rugs lining the floor.

"Well, Jane," she said, stretching her knotted muscles, "this is the day of Nan's wedding. I had best start dressing; I mustn't be late, and I mustn't look a fright, even though I slept poorly indeed. Call the others so that we may begin."

"Yes, your Grace." Jane went to the heavy door, throwing the latch and summoning Elizabeth's other tiring-women, who were sleeping on pallets in the corridor. Filing into the chamber, the women set about preparing Elizabeth for the day ahead. First on was a blood-red kirtle, closely fitted. A gown of black and gold was drawn over it, cinched at the middle with a decorative belt to accentuate the waist. A transparent partlet covered the plunging neckline for modesty. Jane combed out her long dark hair and then braided it, while one of the other ladies, Christian, attached her hennin and *cointoise* veil.

Jane held up a looking glass to let Elizabeth see how she looked. The Dowager Duchess eyed her reflection critically. She had lost much weight since John died—her body leaner, her face tending to gauntness. Years ago, when she was bearing Anne, she had been inclined to plumpness. John Paston, a foolish young fop if there ever was one, had escorted her to her lodgings at Yarmouth, fawning over her and attempting to make conversation—which went rather poorly as he knew not how to flatter a lady and only managed to insult! He had commented that she was of 'goodly stature with long, large sides' and 'so large, the babe should have room to come out easily!'

She had chastised the silly fellow for his unintended insult and sent him away so that she might have some peace, but Elizabeth had heard from her servants that Paston was sorely dismayed by her coolness and left scratching his head about what he had done wrong.

Men... Elizabeth sighed as her ladies powdered her face with the root of the Madonna Lily and reddened her cheeks with unguents crafted from Angelica leaves. She would never marry again. She had wed John at five summers, the same age as Anne, and she desired no other husband. In her widowhood, she would stay available to Anne should she be needed.

Dressed and perfumed, she was as ready as she would ever be for the long day ahead. She set off to find her daughter, who had been whisked away to the Queen's Apartments the night before.

When she arrived, she was relieved that the Queen was not there, having left to meet with the King before the commencement of the ceremony in St. Stephen's Chapel. Before she departed, she had given instructions to her ladies-in-waiting, including some of her numerous sisters, to prepare Anne for the wedding.

Elizabeth paused in the doorway, taking in the sight for a few moments. Her daughter stood in a circle of women, the light from the cressets turning her hair a dark, rich reddish colour like the finest wine. She wore a gown of blue silk, the colour preferred for wedding dresses because of its association with the Virgin, and a short cloak over it, rich red velvet and ermine, sewn with the Rose en Soleil. A silver circlet sparkling with gems pushed her locks away from her forehead. However, despite her sumptuous garments and her bravely straight posture, her expression was one of nervous bewilderment.

"Mama!" she cried, catching sight of Elizabeth, and she would have rushed to Elizabeth's side, save that one of the women caught her by the arm and held her back.

"Princesses do not run, my Lady Anne," said the woman, one of the Queen's sisters, Martha.

Elizabeth bit the inside of her cheek to keep herself from rushing to Anne's defence. As if the Woodville women knew what it was like to be a princess or even noble. Their mother, Jacquetta, was of high breeding, her father the Count of St. Pol, and her mother, Margaret of Baux, a descendant of Eleanor, a daughter of King John, but she had a chequered past, secretly marrying a man of much lower status after her husband, the Duke of Bedford, died. It had caused a great scandal at the time.

Secret marriages… It seemed the Woodvilles were rather fond of them.

"Is the Lady Anne ready?" asked Elizabeth, keeping her voice as steady as she could. "I believe it is nearly time. The celebrants have arrived in the courtyard; they are now entering the chapel."

Martha glanced over at a large hourglass sitting on a table, trickles of sand filtering through its narrow waist into the bulb below. "Is it as late as that? Yes, yes, we must not tarry longer." She grasped a comb and swept it through Anne's hair, making the child gasp as she tugged on a snarl. "Don't fret so, Lady Anne! You want to look fit to marry a prince, do you not?"

Elizabeth glanced away, scarcely able to control herself. Behind her silk, velvet and tulle rustled as the Woodville women and other attendants prepared to leave the chamber.

Accompanied by high-ranking members of the Queen's household, the bridal party processed towards St. Stephen's Chapel. They were joined by the Queen's brother, the suave, learned Anthony Woodville, and the handsome young Earl of Lincoln, a nephew to the King, who took positions on either side of Anne, who walked alone, swathed in her finery, looking more like an overdressed poppet than an actual bride. Elizabeth found herself almost at the rear of the procession, struggling to keep an eye on her daughter as the Woodville sisters streamed in front of her, clearly jockeying for the best positions.

Arriving at the chapel door, James Goldwell, the Bishop of Lincoln, resplendent in cope and tall mitre, greeted the wedding procession with a stern, upraised hand. "Halt!" he commanded. "There is an impediment, and the marriage ceremony cannot continue. Lady Anne and the Lord Richard are related within forbidden degrees."

The party stopped, silent, heads bowed. This revelation by the Bishop was all theatre, for a dispensation to permit the marriage had been duly applied for months before, as all in the procession knew well. The halt was merely to enable high-ranking churchmen to give confirmation of the legality of the marriage in front of those attending the ceremony.

Sure enough, Doctor Gunthorpe, the Canon of St. Stephen's and Dean of the Chapel Royal, emerged from the chapel with a scroll in hand. Unrolling it, he cleared his throat and read in a ringing voice, "Given upon the 4th of May, St. Peter's, Rome, by His Holiness Pope Sixtus IV:

To Edward, King of England, dispensation at the petition of the King and also of his son, Richard, Duke of York, and Anne de Mowbray of the diocese of Norwich, infants, for the said Richard and Anne who have completed their fifth and fourth years of age respectively to contract espousals forthwith, and as soon as they reach the lawful age to contract marriage, notwithstanding that they are related in the third and fourth degrees of kindred. Oblate Nobis.

The Bishop and Canon then stood aside, and the bride, her escorts, and other followers were admitted into the chapel. Sweet incense burned in censers, sending fragrant vapours coiling around the fan-vaulted ceiling. Everywhere hung decorative banners and azure tappets embroidered with golden Fleur de Lys and hundreds of expensive candles burned brightly.

The King and Queen were already there, seated beneath a canopy of cloth of gold. Some of their children were with them, three fair-faced little princesses with waving golden hair and the heir, the Prince of Wales, tall for his age and favouring his father's side of the family. The little bridegroom, Prince Richard, stood slightly to one side, next to the Dowager Duchess Cecily, mother to the King.

Elizabeth's gaze was drawn to the boy, not having seen him for several years. He was a handsome child, probably more so than his older brother, whose face was longer and paler. Richard was sandy-haired and smiling, with a noticeable dimple in his chin, but as he turned, Elizabeth noticed a slight droop to one of his eyelids. It marred his good looks a little, but she remembered that it was a family trait that passed through the Plantagenet bloodline, sometimes skipping generations before it appeared again.

Smiling with surprising gentleness, Anthony Woodville held out his hand to Anne. The girl glanced over at her mother, wordlessly asking permission, and Elizabeth nodded, a lump in her throat. Shyly, Anne took hold of Anthony's hand as he led her over to her groom, who eyed her with curiosity, just as he might a new puppy or pony.

King Edward rose from his seat and stood before the little bride, a glittering figure in rich purple and ermine, rings sparkling on every finger, and a huge chain of jewelled suns and roses around his neck. "Come," he said to Anne, "I shall walk you up the aisle."

The King's huge hand enclosed the child's, and together they processed slowly in the direction of the high altar and the Bishop of Norwich, who was officiating over the ceremony. Prince Richard walked on the other side of his sire, unescorted.

Taking her place across from the royal family, Elizabeth watched as the Mass was spoken and the vows were taken. Her eyes blurred at times, though from tears or through anguish she could not tell, and she could not hear the words spoken, though she knew them well enough herself. She wondered if, in the future, Nan would recall this day with fondness or not. Or even remember it. She struggled to remember her own childhood wedding to John—nothing but distant recollections of candles, murmured prayers, and wall paintings wreathed in candle smoke.

The nuptial Mass finally ended. Two great Dukes, resplendent in gleaming samite robes and wearing ducal coronets, stepped forward to distribute coins to those within the church and to the folk clamouring outside the chapel in the palace courtyard.

Elizabeth recognised them at once. One was Richard of Gloucester, the King's youngest sibling. She knew him as the loyal brother who had gone into exile with Edward when the Earl of Warwick restored old King Henry to the throne and Edward's crown seemed lost. Slight and lean, of average height but with almost delicate arms and legs, he bore little resemblance to his mighty brother, although, as the light of the cressets stroked down his clean-shaven cheek, there was a little similarity here and there.

The other Duke was almost completely the opposite of Gloucester. Harry Stafford, Duke of Buckingham, husband of the Queen's sister, Katherine—a union he was said to scorn, for she was not of high enough breeding for his taste, even if she was sister to a queen consort. Harry was a finger's breadth taller than Richard, his hair a dusty golden brown and curling, worn tighter and less lengthy than the other Duke. Whereas Gloucester's garments were of an almost inky blue, patterned with golden thread, Buckingham's samite was a vivid, almost acidic green, shot through with tawny slashes and decorated with his emblem in silver—the twisted Stafford knot.

Returning to the chapel from his distribution of largesse, the Dukes prepared to escort Nan from St. Stephen's Chapel. Gloucester leaned over and took her arm, and with Buckingham on the opposite side, began the grand procession to the King's Great Chamber, where the nuptial feast would be served. The King and Queen left their seats, and accompanied by their newly married son and other children, followed after the Dukes in great state, surrounded by some of the highest nobles in the land— William Hastings, Lord Stanley and his wife, Margaret Beaufort, Earl John of Lincoln, Anthony Woodville, the Queen's sons Thomas and Richard Grey from her first marriage, the Bourchiers, the Fitz Alans, the Herberts and others she knew less well.

Elizabeth was drawn into the procession by Buckingham's wife, a pretty woman, though an earthier, less ethereal attractiveness than her queenly sister. She was heavy with child, although her gown hid most of her shape. "Come, Elizabeth," she said. "It would not be fitting for you to be at the raggle-taggle end of the procession, since your daughter is the bride. You and I shall walk together. I pray you help me if I stumble, for this babe I carry makes it impossible for me to see my feet!"

Elizabeth smiled wanly at Katherine, glad of her congeniality on this emotional day.

"And you shall, of course, sit with Harry and me," Katherine Woodville continued, "at the high table, as is your right."

Elizabeth must have looked relieved, despite her best efforts to keep a cool, austere appearance, for Katherine gave a high tinkling laugh and informally patted her sleeve. "You did not think you were going to spend the banquet in the kitchens with the servants, did you? Fear not. My sister would never permit such a thing. Bess…I mean, the Queen likes propriety."

Words tumbled from Elizabeth's lips before she had time to mull them over. "I fear her Grace does not like me overmuch, or so it seemed when we spoke."

Katherine Woodville stared at Elizabeth then laughed again. "My sister does put on airs—as well she might, being queen—but she is not as fierce as she sometimes appears, Duchess Elizabeth. You will grow used to her ways and she to you yours, I am certain. You are family now, and to us Woodvilles, family is everything."

As Elizabeth and Katherine reached the arched door leading into the banqueting hall, Duke Richard came up to them, having seen the bride comfortably seated at the high table next to her new husband. Both children were propped high on tasselled pillows, for they were too small to easily reach their trenchers without them.

"My Lady, may I escort you to the high table?" Richard asked Elizabeth, giving her a smile. He was of a much more solemn disposition than his brother the King, and his smile was a surprise, opening his face and accentuating his youth. She found herself staring into his deep blue-grey eyes, then modestly dropped her gaze to the tiled floor. He was comelier than she had thought when not obscured by his more flamboyant kinsmen.

Katherine nudged her, and Elizabeth nodded to the Duke. "You may, my Lord of Gloucester."

Duke Richard guided her to her place, next to Harry Stafford. He then sat on her other side. The newlywed children were seated in the middle of the table, with the King, Queen and their other children surrounding them, all under exquisite silk canopies. Trestle tables stretched away down the hall, the topmost presided over by Thomas Grey, the Marquis of Dorset, and Margaret Beaufort, Lady Stanley. Dressed in rich black, a rosary of green glass beads clacking on her girdle, the small, bone-thin Margaret had the appearance of a very wealthy nun. A wealthy nun with shrewd, intelligent eyes, who missed nothing that was going on in the room.

With the celebrants all gathered and in their allotted places, troupes of the finest minstrels began wandering into the hall, the sound of drums, shawms, and pipes rising up to ring in the rafters. Tumblers and saltatrixes somersaulted in next, dressed in elaborate costumes and masks. They sprang high in the air and vaulted over each other's backs, twirling and spinning with almost preternatural agility. Dressed in patchwork yellow and green, John Scogan, Edward's Fool, darted among the celebrants before rolling head over heels along the edge of the High Table, the bells on his cap and shoes jingling merrily, before spinning off to the centre of the floor and juggling a handful of silver balls. He aimed one at Lord Stanley's head, much to the amusement of all, but when Stanley glared with a look of menace in his eyes, the Fool quickly spun around and bounced it off the head of a passing page instead.

Scogan's tomfoolery over, the first course of the banquet was brought from the great kitchens of the palace. Normally this would consist of *salat*, but fresh greens were sparse at that time of the year, so it was mushroom tarts and *mackerouns*, accompanied by milk mixed with red wine, sugars, and spices, which would 'open the belly' for further delights to come.

Elizabeth drank cautiously and pushed food around her plate while glancing aside to watch how Nan was coping. She was relieved to see the little girl had grown much more animated and was chatting with Prince Richard and his sisters and even with the King, who seemed quite amused by her chatter. The

Queen, however, sat in stern hauteur, shining with a silver radiance, like an austere Madonna.

Duke Richard, noticing where Elizabeth's gaze rested, nodded. "The Princess, she will be well tended, Duchess, have no fear."

"Every mother fears for her child, your Grace," she said wryly.

"And every father too, especially when he has but one child." Gloucester was suddenly thoughtful. "My boy Ned... I must admit when I am long away from Middleham, his well-being does play on my mind. He has many childish ailments, but then so did I when I was his age. My Lady Mother said my life was often despaired of, yet here I am."

"Forgive me; I had forgotten that you and my cousin Anne have but one child, even as I do. Most assuredly, I will pray to God for his good health...and for Anne's too. How does she fare? It would have soothed me to see her here."

He sighed. "She is indisposed, alas. Like little Edward, she is often plagued by maladies, although she seldom complains. So strange, since her father had the strength of ten; he could ride through the night and then do battle..." He trailed off, staring into his trencher.

Elizabeth pretended to dab her lips with her white linen napkin. She knew the Duke had spent time in the Earl of Warwick's household as a boy before Richard Neville turned his coat and went over to the Lancastrian side. She suspected young Gloucester may have seen Neville as something of a replacement for his father, the Duke of York, who had died at Wakefield when Richard was but a boy. Until the Earl rebelled, of course, appalled by Edward's secret marriage to Elizabeth Woodville and the embarrassment of the King rejecting Bona of Savoy, with whom Warwick had been brokering a match. Then any kindly feelings Gloucester held must surely have turned to hate, especially when the Earl married Anne to Margaret of Anjou's son. But those times lay in the past. Warwick, that overmighty subject, fell at Barnet and was now entombed beneath cold stone at Bisham Abbey. And Anne, widowed only months after becoming a wife to Edward of Lancaster, had married Richard instead.

Suddenly Elizabeth wondered if Richard *knew*. Knew about Eleanor and her entanglement with the King. He was close with Edward; it was always possible that the King had divulged the truth in an unguarded moment…

Wine loosening her tongue, she made to speak—Jesu, it would be so good to unburden herself to someone! But thankfully sanity struck before her tongue began to wag, and her mind screeched, enraged: *What are you doing, you feckless fool?*

Feigning a cough, she pulled back, horrified at what she had almost revealed.

Of course, Gloucester would not know. He would have only been a lad of about ten when Edward met Eleanor at her manor of Burton Dassett. And it was unlikely Edward, even in the worst moments of indiscretion, would ever mention such a thing, as the consequences for his family would be terrible.

"Are you well, Duchess Elizabeth?" Richard turned to her, hearing her cough. "Can I get you more…more wine?"

"Yes, thank you, my Lord Duke," she murmured, although she thought more alcohol was the last thing she needed. She dabbed at her lips again; traces of wine stained the white cloth like smears of blood. Richard beckoned to a page boy, who lifted an ornate silver ewer and poured Elizabeth another goblet of Rhenish. She took it gratefully, though she raised it to her lips without drinking; it was a shield to hide behind.

Fortunately, the next course of the feast was arriving to a blare of horns and a troupe of jongleurs singing. An acrobat turned three cartwheels before the high table, then halted, standing on tiptoes, his lean body contorted into an almost unnatural position. He wore tight red hose and his torso was painted scarlet; a mask clung to his face, redolent of the devils in Doom Scenes painted above many a church chancel. One of his colleagues skipped out from the sidelines, bowing as he handed him a burning torch. The crimson mummer whirled around three times and then lunged forward as if about to eat the brand he carried. Almost all the wedding celebrants gasped in alarm. But the torch did not enter his mouth but rather ignited some strange potion he held therein, Eyes glittering in the crimson mask, he belched out a long streak of flame before the King and Queen's seats. The children present all screamed and then, as the actor pranced away, burst into high-pitched laughter, pretending they were not the least bit afraid of the fiery devil.

In streamed the food in the wake of the fire-eater. *Tartes de chare* pork pie, stuffed capon, sturgeon cooked in vinegar and sprinkled with ginger, veal loin, and a civet of hare, accompanied by *Cruste Rolles* cooked in a pan, ideal for mopping up the rich gravies poured over the meat.

Elizabeth picked at the food, wondering why it all seemed to taste of ashes and dust. She fanned her face; the room had grown very hot and extremely loud. She wished the night would hurry up and pass. It was hard to feign merriment for hours on end. At least Little Nan seemed to be enjoying herself.

The acrobats and tumblers vanished into side passages, and a different troupe of minstrels appeared, clad in the murrey and blue of the House of York and wearing pewter boar badges on their doublets.

"These are my musicians, Duchess Elizabeth," said Richard of Gloucester. "I asked the King if he would allow them to play at the wedding and he agreed. I take them with me wherever I travel. Music soothes my soul when it is troubled by hardship and pain."

Elizabeth glanced at her dining companion. She wondered what pain he referred to—spiritual pain or pain of the body. She had heard whispers that he was not well-made, but in his finely tailored attire he looked well enough. "I also feel solace in music. I pray that your musicians' talents can bring me ease."

Richard regarded her for a few long seconds. Her cheeks began to burn under his scrutiny. "Yes," the Duke said slowly, "I pray so too."

The musicians were drawing nigh to the foot of the table, playing on psaltery, vielle, sackbut, and drum. They bowed to the King and Queen, to the royal children and Little Nan, to Duke Richard, to the King's mother Cecily and to the Duke of

Buckingham. Afterwards, they began to play a lively dance tune, beckoning the young royal couple to join them on the floor.

Edward laughed and ushered Prince Richard and Anne onto the floor of the hall. Despite her youth, Anne had taken a few rudimentary dance lessons, as befitted a noble maiden, but Richard had not had a single one, for he was still in the nursery, and the main bulk of his education, when he would learn the manners and rituals of court life, was yet to begin..

Despite his lack of courtly training, a big grin spread across the little prince's face as he trundled onto the floor to the sound of furious clapping. Not shy in the least, he began to jump and jig in his fine velvet wedding clothes, his dark golden curls bobbing and his bonnet flying off. The wedding guests laughed uproariously at this, as did King Edward; even Elizabeth Woodville broke into a smile, making her look far more approachable.

Enjoying the attention, Richard began to twirl even more wildly, careering from one end of the hall to the other. He had quite forgotten about Anne, who extended her hand to him in a polite attempt to bring him into the dance, but he ignored her and continued on in his rambunctious manner. He was like a shining star, while Anne was a veiled moon, waning. Her face puckered as she fought back tears, knowing not what move to do next.

"This dance was not intended for children's play," Gloucester murmured, within Elizabeth's hearing. "My nephew is of blood royal and should behave as such, not like a dancing ape shipped in for the amusement of the court."

Fortunately, King Edward stepped in at that moment, striding from his high seat, catching up the little prince in his arms and carrying him back to his seat. Several of the Queen's sisters ran out to escort Anne back onto the dais.

"Let us continue." Richard stood up; although he was not as imposing as the King, still he bore an air of authority. "A dance in honour of the bride and groom. May they have good health, and in time, may their union be harmonious, fruitful, and blessed. Duchess Elizabeth…?"

Elizabeth went onto the floor with the Duke, followed by Harry Stafford and his wife, despite her heavy belly, and then others of the nobility. Margaret Beaufort was noticeably absent from the dance, sitting rod-straight on her bench and solemn-faced, as if she did not quite approve of frivolities like dancing.

As the dancing commenced, the tune now more stately than frantic and merry, Duke Richard leaned towards Elizabeth. "I hope you will forgive my brother for that little scene with her children…"

"He is the King," said Elizabeth, a little more sharply than she intended. "There is nought to forgive, my Lord Duke."

"That may be so, but he was, perhaps, not quite himself when he permitted such an unseemly show. He has much on his mind that he cloaks in a false show of merriment."

A shadow passed over Gloucester's face, and Elizabeth guessed he referred to George of Clarence, the middle brother, the *problem* brother, who would be tried before his peers on the morrow. It struck her as odd that King Edward had chosen such a day for the trial so soon after his second son's marriage. Was he giving some kind of veiled warning to those gathered for the nuptials and for the opening of parliament that would follow? One day in the bosom of the family, the next day, should you oppose Edward, on the block? George of Clarence certainly deserved punishment for all his misdeeds, but a King threatening to execute his own brother for treason? She doubted it would come to that, though, no matter what men whispered; no doubt George would merely have a long stay in the Tower, learning to temper his behaviour behind a barred door.

It must be difficult for Duke Richard, not knowing what the King might rule on the morrow. He was close in age to Clarence, and they had fared abroad together as children, exiles in the wake of their sire's death in battle. Even if events had separated them, surely a bond, no matter how fragile, still remained.

Her own thoughts travelled back to Eleanor, dying at her house in Kenninghall, where Elizabeth would soon take up residence. Dying alone while she was feasting and carousing in Burgundy at Margaret of York's nuptials. Suddenly, she wanted, *needed* to ask Richard just one question, nought more. "Did you ever meet my sister, Eleanor?" Her words tumbled out, breathy, strained.

"I cannot say I ever did." He shook his head lightly. The jewel on his bonnet winked red in the candlelight. "Why do you ask?"

"It…it…" Elizabeth felt blood rush to her head, and again the fear of revealing too much swept over her. "I just wondered," she said awkwardly, "if Anne had ever written to her…perhaps when I was away at the Duchess of Burgundy's marriage. Eleanor died around that time. I was still abroad. It was a great shock."

"That would be around ten years ago," said Richard. "The year Ned…I mean, his Grace the King, sent the Herberts into Wales to break the siege of Harlech. It lasted seven years! The year when tensions grew between my brother and Warwick. I knew Anne from my time at Middleham, but she was very young then and I dared not write her, nor she me—already the King had warned me and George that the Neville maidens were not for us. Warned us…with a threat of imprisonment."

"I see." Elizabeth bowed her head. She knew Edward would make good on his threats.

"If Anne ever had correspondence with Eleanor, she has never mentioned it to me, but it seems unlikely owing to her youth at the time."

"Of course. I forget myself—Anne would have been scarcely more than a child when my sister's soul was received into God's keeping." And Eleanor would have never told her secret to anyone whose ability to be discrete was unknown.

"It is hard to lose members of one's family," said Richard, and a worried expression crossed his face again. Elizabeth instinctively knew he once again thought of George, incarcerated in the Tower as he awaited trial.

The tempo of the music changed again, growing faster and livelier. The dancers moved upon the tiled floor like pieces on a chessboard, changing partners, and suddenly Richard had stepped back a pace and another man was looming over Elizabeth, clearing his throat.

The Duke of Buckingham, Harry Stafford.

Stafford's large face, not unattractive but rather fleshy and made platter-wide by his grin, floated close to Elizabeth's. The scent of the musk he wore in great abundance washed over her. "Would you care to partner me in the next roundel, Duchess? Katherine is too great with child to join in, and I would be sorely displeased not to stretch my limbs on the dance floor. I am a skilled dancer, am I not, Gloucester?"

"If you say so, Harry," said Gloucester, bemused. "Although I do not think I have had the, ah, pleasure of witnessing it."

Stafford's meaty hand swiped down Elizabeth's arm. "Surely you will not turn me down, my Lady?"

Elizabeth had no wish to make enemies for no good reason; Buckingham seemed the type of man who would hold a grudge if he felt his dignity had been offended in any way. "Lead away, my Lord Duke," she said to Stafford, resigned to the dance as the Duke of Gloucester returned to his bench.

The dance seemed to go on for hours, but it likely took less time than a thin slice melting off the top of a candle-clock. Stafford yattered on constantly about himself and his castle at Brecknock, which he found too cold, too small, and too old-fashioned; he even complained to her about his wife being a Woodville, which was rather unwise considering the chamber was brimming with them. She sympathised with Duchess Katherine; she had shown herself the kindest of the Woodville brood and had done well in coming to court so close to her travail. She decided Henry Stafford was most ungallant and vainglorious.

"The King has never sought out my talents," Buckingham continued, as he danced away from her, then reached for her arm and jerked her forward, close to him, making her stumble. "It is most unfair. Still, tomorrow…" he almost seemed to salivate, "Edward has granted me the role of High Steward. Gloucester should have been the one to take the role, but the King won't burden his own brother with that. I, Harry Buckingham, shall proclaim the sentence on fickle, foolish George of Clarence…and will enjoy every moment of it!

His talk was now in dangerous territory; it was also ridiculous. Buckingham actually *reminded* Elizabeth of George of Clarence, albeit an overstuffed, portly George, and at least Clarence had genuinely loved her cousin Isabel Neville, taking no mistresses throughout their marriage and becoming crazed with sorrow when she died.

"Sir…" She managed to withdraw her hand from Stafford's sweaty, beringed paw. "Your enthusiastic dancing has tired me to the point I feel quite faint. I fear I must sit down awhile."

An angry little tic moved the corner of Stafford's mouth, but he forced himself to smile. It did not reach his eyes.

This man is dangerous, Elizabeth thought with a sudden jolt. *He looks as if he would gladly strike me.*

"Ah, what a pity," said Buckingham, grin rigid, his gaze challenging. "I fear you do me wrong, Duchess. Whoever shall finish this dance with me?"

"Try Lady Stanley!" she snapped, nodding towards the diminutive figure of Margaret Beaufort, who was picking at her platter as her ever-watchful gaze darted about the hall.

Henry Stafford sputtered in indignation, "My Aunt? But she does not…" and Elizabeth made her escape, gliding effortlessly between the servers bringing in the final course of the banquet. As she returned to her bench beside Gloucester, she saw, to her surprise, that despite his protestations, Buckingham was indeed talking to Margaret Beaufort, although they made no move towards the dance floor. The little woman was conversing with some animation, her face fervent, as if she were possessed by religious ecstasy. Elizabeth guessed she was talking about her son, Henry, who dwelt in exile with his uncle, Jasper Tudor. Elizabeth had heard Henry was Margaret's favourite subject.

"Harry and Lady Stanley are close kin." Richard stared over at the garrulous Buckingham, who was waving his arms as he tried to twist the conversation over to something he preferred— probably himself. "She is his aunt through marriage to his uncle

Henry Stafford, but also close blood kin. His mother, another Margaret Beaufort, was the daughter of Edmund Beaufort and hence is Lady Stanley's cousin."

"It is the most animated I have seen her all evening. I could not fail to notice how sombre she was in demeanour and dress. Almost as if this is a funeral rather than a wedding."

Elizabeth grimaced a little at her own words. She certainly felt little of the joy that was supposed to come as a bride's mother. However, she told herself that possibly one day in the future happiness would emerge from Anne's marriage. Her daughter was now royalty, her sons would be great princes of the realm. Elizabeth must accept that reality and look to a joyous future, even if true joy was at that time in short supply.

Richard and Elizabeth ceased their discussion of Margaret Beaufort as the clarions sounded and the final course of the wedding banquet carried in and placed upon the tables—sweet marchpane and custard tarts, fruit stewed in hippocras, Prince-briskets flecked with caraway seeds, *Blaunched Fritours,* and a series of wondrous subtleties in various shapes, some crafted specifically to delight the royal children—a great, green dragon sporting outstretched sugared wings, a white sugar angel whose hair was streaked with dripping honey, a castle with red-peaked, jelly towers that wobbled as it was brought in on a vast silver tray. There were cries of delight and clapping, and the firebreather returned to dance again and blow more flames into the fuggy air.

Elizabeth noted that Harry Buckingham had returned to his seat after his conversation with Lady Margaret. Fortunately, the Duke seemed to have lost interest in her after her apparent 'snub' and was tucking into the *Fritours*, marchpane, and hippocras with almost indecent gusto.

She glanced over at little Nan, who had forgotten, as children often did, the earlier embarrassment on the dance floor and was nibbling on part of the angel subtlety, sharing the best bits with her new husband, Prince Richard. Her face was weary, though, and her eyes circled by dark rings. The hour was late, too late for ordinary children to be up, but Anne was no longer an ordinary child. She was the wife of a prince of the realm.

As if reading her thoughts, Edward heaved himself out of his carven chair, a little worse for wear, signalling that the feast was over. None of the celebrants could leave until he and the Queen had departed for the night.

Elizabeth Woodville laid down her napkin after dabbing her fine little lips and, light as gossamer, got to her feet, attended by her ladies. Nursemaids filed in to take charge of the children and lead them back to their quarters. Anne went with the others, stiff in her finery, although not without first casting a worried backward glance at her mother.

Katherine Woodville had also risen to her feet, awkwardly holding her big belly. Harry failed to notice, as he continued to indulge in leftover sweetmeats and other fancies, his sharp tongue warning off the servers who had brought in the voiders for collection of discarded food that would later go to the poor.

"You can go to attend the Princess Anne, Duchess," Katherine said, close to Elizabeth's ear. "My sister the Queen truly does not expect you to leave your daughter so soon."

"Oh, thank you." Elizabeth climbed from her bench. "I am afraid I have been away from court so long all of the old protocol is half-forgotten. It is like learning all over again. And, of course, I never expected to have a daughter so…so…" She halted, hesitant, words deserting her.

"Blessed?" said Katherine, brightly.

"Yes. Yes, that is it. *Blessed*," Elizabeth murmured. Fervently, she hoped it would be so…in time.

Gloucester politely stood back from his seat to allow Elizabeth passage. "It was a pleasure to speak with you, Duchess."

"And you, your Grace. Will you be here for the joust next week that will complete the marriage celebrations?"

"Jousts are not among my favourite sports; a waste of good men and better horses, often." Gloucester smiled wryly. "I leave such showy affairs to the likes of Anthony Woodville. I may have left London by the date of the joust—I have not yet decided. Much will depend on tomorrow's outcome…"

The trial. George's trial.

"I pray all goes as you hope, my Lord Duke," said Elizabeth, and she meant it. She cared not a jot for the fate of Clarence, who was at the very least a fool and at worst a traitor or outright insane, but she found herself warming to the youngest York brother. Unkind gossips sometimes name him 'the runt of York's litter,' owing to his smaller size and subdued nature, but in her estimation, beauty without substance like Edward's and a glib tongue that breathed lies through silver like George were meaningless.

Richard's smile was wan. "Pray is all I can do. If we do not meet again in London, I wish you a safe journey to your home. When I have returned to Middleham, I will tell Anne that she must write to you."

"Duchess Elizabeth…please come!" Katherine Woodville was standing in the doorway of the hall, beckoning. "I will guide you to the children's quarters. The party is well on its way there, but in my state, it will be hard to keep pace."

Elizabeth gave a polite curtsey to the Duke of Gloucester and hurried after the Duchess of Buckingham. The cool air in the corridor outside the banquet chamber felt soothing on her face, but now she could not pretend it was the smoke from the fires that made her eyes shed tears.

The final festivities of Little Nan and Prince Richard's wedding took place in a large open space near Westminster Abbey. Stands were set up and pennants and flags raised to announce the presence of all the royal and noble guests. There were images of black eagles and blue and white boars, ferocious bulls and lions of every shade and shape, alongside tangles of knots and chevrons, stars and suns, ships and cups. A lodge, separate from the stands and comfortably furnished and draped in a gorgeous array of silks, was also erected to house the royal family and their special guests.

Elizabeth was invited to the lodge, sitting a few rows behind King Edward and his Queen. Little Nan had a position of prime importance—for on this day, she would outshine even her royal-blooded husband, for she had been designated as the High Princess of the Feast. Around her clustered her new sisters-in-law and aunts by marriage, forming a 'council' of women as found in the old tales of King Arthur's court. Their job was to assist her in judging the outcome of the joust, in which six 'defenders', known as the Party Within, would battle the 'challengers' known as the Party Without.

Elizabeth leaned forward, peering into the bright, wintry sunshine to view the jousting knights. She recognised the Queen's sons by her first marriage, Thomas Grey and Richard Grey, and her brothers, Edward and Anthony, and also Sir Thomas Fynes, Richard Haute, and Robert Clifford. The rest she did not know. She wondered if the Greys and Woodvilles would unite as either challengers or defenders—there were four of them, so they nearly formed one complete side already!

Elizabeth glanced over at her daughter, seated on a gilded throne decorated with goldwork and upholstered with velvet. Her hair flowed loose beneath a circlet, the light catching on its deep red highlights, and her gown, fashioned of a pallid sky-blue brocade shot through with dusky-gold samite, shimmered with hundreds of tiny white gemstones shaped into roses. She appeared far happier and calmer than the week before, especially as her new sister-in-law, Elizabeth of York, stood stalwartly at her side, watching over her and showing her how a princess should behave.

It was easy to pretend that England on that day was all full of light and happiness, especially its royal family, dressed in their best, sipping hippocras and eating wafers in the comfort of the lodge. But there was an edge in the air, a sense of unease despite the brazen trumpets, heralds in bright surcoats, and dignitaries from afar clad in exotic finery.

The unease radiated down from the White Tower, adamant and unforgiving on the spreading banks of the turgid Thames, where George of Clarence was still imprisoned after his trial. And he would always remain there...until his death. Edward had done the unthinkable, something no king in living memory had ever done—he had found his brother guilty of high treason and thus condemned to die. Buckingham had gloatingly read out the death sentence. Word on the street was that Duchess Cecily had screamed and begged for her middle son's life, but Edward had regarded her coldly, with no pity, for all that she was his mother. "My Queen was afraid that should George live, our eldest son would never come to the throne!" he told her. "Did you want to see that, madam? George was so debased he even hired some charlatan of an astrologer to tell him that 'G' would soon hold the reins of power!"

It was as if the House of York was tearing itself apart after striving so hard to reach the throne.

Elizabeth focused on the list field where the combatants had gathered after exiting their painted pavilions. Gaudy plumes waved on helmets; bright caparisons rippled on the frames of their horses. Soon the lists resounded to the clash of weapons against burnished armour and the thunder of horses' hooves in mad gallop. The crowd was in a near-frenzy, various sections cheering on their favourites, then groaning in torment when their chosen knight was unhorsed.

The constant passing of the knights became a blur to Elizabeth, as the sunlight sparking off swords and cuirasses brought a sharp headache to her temples. The air reeked of London—a mingling of beasts, the rank Thames, the heads spiked above the gates. The crowd, too, bothered her with its endless roaring and weeping. It was perhaps *too* enthusiastic, as if it were an attempt to blot out the rift in the House of York, to forget the gossip of the St. Paul's Walkers, who had spread the word in every tavern, every bear pit, that the King was going to execute his own brother. As faithless as George of Clarence had been, surely committing such a violent act on one's blood kin was still deemed wicked, taboo, an echo of Cain and Abel?

Out on the lists, Thomas Grey went down with a crash, his legs and arms flailing in the air. A disappointed shout went up from the Queen's Woodville kin; the Queen herself made no sound and sat still as a stone next to Edward, Prince of Wales, Prince Richard, and Nan, but her mouth folded down in a glower of disappointment. The King himself appeared on edge, bags beneath his eyes, his usual enthusiasm at such spectacles curbed, no doubt by the enormity of his decision regarding Clarence. Elizabeth wondered if Richard of Gloucester had left the city for Yorkshire as he had suggested he might; certes, he was not here at the joust.

Before the grand royal lodge, a lance broke with a resounding crack, and a body cartwheeled through the air and fell to the ground with a loud 'whump' that brought almost everyone to their feet, even the King and Queen. There were some very distraught cries from the Queen's sisters and ladies-in-waiting; it was Anthony Woodville who had fallen, unhorsed by Thomas Fynes.

Fortunately, Woodville was unhurt, staggering to his feet and removing his helmet so all the spectators could see he was well. "What on earth is wrong with our brother?" the Queen snapped at her sisters, who looked dour and shook their heads. "He has shamed us today, as has Thomas. You know how many assembled here love nought more than to see our family fail. It amuses them."

"No one can win every tourney," said Katherine, Duchess of Buckingham, quite cheery despite her brother's tumble.

The Queen's green-eyed glare made her sister take a step back. Next to his mother, the Prince of Wales looked dismayed and bit his lip. "We *always* win…one way or another, Kate," Elizabeth hissed at her sister, and then she turned away, calling for a goblet of claret and a dish of fritters and sweetmeats.

All eyes swivelled back to the lists as the combatants gathered again—this time on foot with swords. The sound of blade clanging against blade filled the air, and once again, the stands were full of scarcely bridled excitement.

In the end, it was Robert Clifford who stood triumphant, his opponent fallen heavily on his back, while shouting, "I yield, I yield!"

Edward raised himself from his throne, an enormous figure in royal purple and ermine. "Well done, well done all!" he cried in a great voice, "I think we have all won today…and everyone is still alive!" He let out a boom of laughter, but somehow it felt forced, and there was no sparkle of mirth in his eyes. The King's mind was clearly on other matters—family matters.

He then gestured to little Anne in the special seat of the Princess of the Joust, decked in royal finery and wreaths of dried flowers reminiscent of a past spring that would soon blossom anew. "Leave now and rest awhile, brave knights of England, who fought for honour this day before my son, Richard, and my daughter-by-marriage, Princess Anne. After Vespers, I bid you come unto the King's Chamber where prizes for the winners of the tourney shall be given by the fair hand of Anne herself."

The crowds roared, clapping in delight. Anne suddenly glanced over at her mother, excited, her warm brown eyes shining.

They clapped for her, the Princess of the Feast! She was someone of importance now. She had a new special family, and because of that, the common folk loved her, wanted to look upon her, to applaud, to bow, to send her gifts.

Elizabeth's heart jolted at Nan's blissful innocence. But a wave of pride swelled within her heart too. Perhaps her fears for the child *were* only a widow's foolishness. There was every chance Anne would be cossetted, protected, and loved in the

Queen's household. She clutched a little silver cross studded with garnets that hung around her neck—a gift to her, years ago, from Eleanor—and prayed silently to the Virgin for her daughter's future, and also for the strength to let her go.

The King's Chamber flickered with the light of a hundred cressets. The paintings on the walls wavered and danced through the tallowy smoke. The palace courtiers gathered round, their goblets overflowing with malmsey and Rhenish, as servants swirled around the tables bearing silver platters full of sweet offerings—dates rolled in crumbs, sugar, and cinnamon; pine nuts on toasted bread, slathered in golden honey—and other small savoury morsels, such as mortrews, cheese-stuffed eggs, and shrimp with fennel seeds.

Maskers and mummers swarmed in, dressed in fantastical costumes—knights from King Arthur's court; Adam and Eve swathed in leaves; wild woodwoses of the forest with antlers upon their heads; the giant Goliath (played by two actors, one sitting atop the other's shoulders); saints and angels with rayed nimbuses made of real candles; bears and wolves who gave out fierce growls and darted at the squealing children in the hall.

On the dais, Little Nan was centre stage again, a slight figure in her gorgeous gown, which had been changed to one of damson taffeta and silk. The King and Queen stood in the shadows, smiling, their two sons beside them. Elizabeth watched from the opposite side of the hall as Anne's attendants, 'the council of ladies' filed up onto the dais.

Princess Elizabeth, her hair shining like molten gold in the flickering light, approached Anne holding an oak box inlaid with cabochons. "High and Mighty Princess of the Feast," she cried in strong, ringing tones, belying her age, "here are the prizes to be bestowed on our most able and competent knights."

Anne took the box and opened it. Carefully, she picked out a golden letter, an A for Anne, studded with a solitary, glittering diamond. The onlookers gave a gasp of awe and pressed forward to the foot of the dais.

A trumpet shouted out a loud tantara, and the mummers ceased their antics and retreated to the back of the chamber, followed by the servers.

In marched the men who had partaken in the joust, refreshed and washed after their efforts, and dressed in sumptuous robes, collars, cloaks and bonnets. They lined up before the dais, while a herald proclaimed, "The winner of the tourney, supreme in jousting and other martial sports—Sir Thomas Fynes, step forward."

Thomas Fynes swept up onto the dais and knelt respectfully before Anne and her chief attendant, Elizabeth of York. "Arise, Sir," said Anne, her voice surprisingly strong, touched only by the smallest quiver. She was clearly trying to emulate her new sister-in-law. "I present unto you the award of a golden letter, one which stands for my name, Anne Mowbray."

Fynes rose and gently took the golden letter from Nan's tiny, delicate fingers. He pressed it to his lips, then turned to the onlookers and, flashing white fire, raised it on high, while cheers rattled the very timbers of the ceiling.

Next came Robert Clifford, who was announced as the winner of swordsmanship at the tourney. Anne bestowed upon him another golden letter, shaped as an 'M' for Mowbray, and studded with a fine red ruby.

Lastly, Richard Haute, tall, lanky, and dark-haired, stepped onto the dais. His prize was for his ability to run fleetly and fight nimbly while wearing full harness. Anne presented him with the last golden letter, this one bearing an emerald. That final letter was an 'E', representing the King, Queen, the Prince of Wales, and the Princess Elizabeth.

But as little Nan handed it to Richard Haute, her gaze drifted over to her watching mother, and Elizabeth knew she had not been forgotten, at least in her daughter's thoughts. 'E' for Elizabeth, mother of the new princess.

And later, as Anne was escorted to her chambers and tucked into bed by her ladies and by Elizabeth, she leaned over to her mother, her loose hair trailing down in a wine-red cascade, and whispered, her large brown eyes intense, "I would have given you a letter, mama, if it was permitted. For I think you are the most wonderful and bravest of them all."

Elizabeth remained in London for a little while after the wedding. It eased her worries to see Nan settling in with the other princesses. The sound of their giggles both brought relief, but also piercing sadness, for soon she must return to her own lands and begin her life as a dowager Duchess.

During the daytime, she visited the mercantile areas of London with her lady-in-waiting, Jane, and the Norfolk men-at-arms who had accompanied her journey from Framlingham. She visited milliners and hatters, cordwainers, and even a goldsmith. She could no longer be extravagant, though, as her income was limited—gone were the days when John allowed her to choose multiple hennins and gowns of samite and taffeta. Now, she carried home a simple headdress, unadorned, and a good quality gown, but one without gems or pearls, or intricate designs sewn in with gold thread. The jewellery she looked at was sighed over but left on the shelf, despite the goldsmith trying to tempt her by lowering the price.

When she was not travelling through the city with Jane, Elizabeth was in the King's court, listening to gossip. Duchess Katherine had departed for Wales with her husband, Harry Stafford, which shocked some as she was very close to her lying-in period. Elizabeth thought it was callous, even brutish, for Stafford to insist they leave since Katherine was so far gone in her pregnancy and there were several Buckingham residences in London where they could reside till the babe was born. It confirmed her opinion that Stafford was a selfish man with an edge of cruelty about him that alienated many, for all that he radiated wealth with his peacock dress and elaborate bonnets. Some said he was a true orator who could charm even a withered beldam into sin or could blag a penny from a poor man, but she knew nought of his shifty tongue. All she remembered was his glittering gaze, full of a hunger she could not name—not lust precisely, at least not carnal lust, but a burning desire for more than he possessed.

She listened in as Martha Woodville began to opine on the same subject. "I pray our sister shall reach Brecknock without incident," she said to another Woodville sister, Jacquetta, Baroness Strange, named after their illustrious and scandalous mother, who had wed a King's brother but, after his death, eloped with a handsome though humble knight without King Henry's permission. "What if our new nephew or niece ends up born in some tavern *en route*? Katherine would be mortified."

"You would think Harry would show more care, especially as he has no heir as yet," sniffed Jacquetta, "but he shows little concern for anyone but himself. He only bears our poor sister because the King says he must. She is but a broodmare to him."

Martha pursed her rosy lips. "Hmm, I dare say that one would like to have wed a blood princess, or a duke's daughter at the very least."

"Well, Edward was having none of it, even when Harry was but a mere boy. Pampered by his grandmother, the boy arrived at court with the worst attitude I have ever seen. Nothing was right for him. You would have thought he was a prince."

Jacquetta smirked. "He considers himself so. Remember how he began to wear the Arms of England unquartered. The heralds permitted it, but he did not ask the King and Edward was not pleased."

"He'll be even less pleased if he learns that Harry has a copy of the decree legitimising the Beauforts...but without the codicil saying that they cannot accede to the throne."

"Surely that's untrue!"

"Katherine told me. She swore me to secrecy—but that secrecy includes *you*, sister. We are a close family, the closest...and hence we have risen from humbleness to the highest pinnacle it is possible to obtain. We must hold back nothing from each other, and we must do what needs to be done to continue in our rise."

Jacquetta laughed. "True, although I am glad that I didn't have to marry Henry Stafford! Though I'd have done my duty, with regrets…"

Troubled, Elizabeth moved away from the Woodville women and retired to her chambers. So she had been right about Buckingham. She was glad he was far away; it was obvious few liked his company, even his cousin the King.

Over the week, though, the court gossip changed, growing darker, more ominous. Most had believed the King would commute George of Clarence's death sentence to lifelong imprisonment, having taught him a harsh lesson. But no word came of any change of heart, and the days rolled on towards the terrible outcome. Tension hung in the air, thick as rancid butter, and Elizabeth began to feel uncomfortable among the courtiers. It was as if a funeral shroud hung over Westminster, its folds drawing in, tightening. No one seemed willing to talk, as the excitement of the royal marriage waned and the death-watch for Clarence began.

Elizabeth tried to visit Nan as much as possible, but she found access was often barred, although in the politest of ways— Anne was having dance lessons, Anne was learning her letters, Anne was having a new gown fitted, Anne was in the Queen's presence and none other could enter.

And then one morning, shortly after Elizabeth had returned from morning prayer, a knock sounded on the door of her chamber, brisk and, to her ears, demanding.

"Jane, see who that is," she told her maid.

Jane scrambled to the door and opened it. In swept a woman Elizabeth recognised, Alice Haute, the wife of Sir John Fogge. Alice had served the Queen as a lady-in-waiting once and was also a distant cousin of the Woodvilles. Although she no longer attended upon the Queen, she remained close to her and frequently visited the court.

"A good day to you, Lady Fogge," said Elizabeth with wary courtesy. She had never liked John Fogge, whom she deemed a shifty sort of fellow, and Alice was aloof and guarded. "I trust all is well?"

"All is well with *me*, Duchess," said Alice, "but I cannot speak for others in London. The Queen fears there may be *trouble* shortly…" She paused, smoothing down a crease in her yellow-and-white brocade. "I am sure you know of what I speak."

Elizabeth gave a curt nod. Clarence's execution.

"My cousin the Queen has therefore decided to move her household to Greenwich Palace, outside the walls of the city. It is most pleasant there, with a large deer park established by Duke Humphrey of Gloucester, and it will provide a safer and more pleasant abode for the royal children, including the Princess Anne."

"I see," said Elizabeth in a soft voice, and then she let silence hang between them like a winding sheet.

Alice Fogge's cheeks pinked, and Elizabeth knew she had correctly guessed the reason for her unexpected visit. The Queen was going to remove to Greenwich Palace with her children—but her plans did not include Elizabeth.

It was time to leave Nan with the royal family and depart for Norfolk to start a new, quiet life at Kenninghall. The life of a Dowager Duchess, filled with piety, prayer, and relative poverty since nearly all her dower lands, sources of her income, had ended up as Anne's according to the marriage agreement. Anne's, although, in truth, the possessions of young Prince Richard.

"Tell her Grace the Queen that I am thankful for her taking my daughter to safety, and that I fully understand the necessity."

"I shall," mumbled Alice Fogge, and she scurried from the chamber, banging the door behind her, clearly anxious to leave Elizabeth's presence.

"Oh, my Lady," began Jane, touching her mistress's arm.

"No, Jane, no tears for me, please," said Elizabeth. "The break must be made, difficult though it might be. Truth be told, I long to leave these busy streets and smell the fresh air of the countryside, to hear cows lowing in the fields instead of caitiffs brawling in the streets."

"I will start packing for your departure then, by your leave," said Jane.

Elizabeth departed the following Thursday on a clear, cool morning with only a few greyish rags of clouds trailing across the sun. The Queen had permitted her to meet with Nan in the gardens before her departure on the long journey to Kenninghall.

Anne looked spritely and well, her cheeks rosy in the chill and her hair haloed by the sunlight. She chattered on about her 'new friends' Princess Elizabeth, so kind and with such pretty red-gold hair, and Mary, who could play the flute, and Cecily, who could sing like an angel.

"I am glad you find good cheer with the King's daughters," said Elizabeth. "How is your husband, Prince Richard?"

"He is a boy." Anne waved her hand dismissively. "But he is not the worst boy I have met. My nurse says she is sure he will be handsome one day, just like King Edward."

Elizabeth smiled. "I am sure he will be, and he will show you great kindness, just like his sisters."

"We are going to a new palace in a few days," Anne chirped, her eyes sparkling with excitement. "Bessie—that's Princess Elizabeth, mama—says it is more beautiful there, not as noisy and right on the riverside, but the river's not as big or as smelly. There is a big park, and I am to have a pony…"

"I am sure you will love it there, my sweetling." Elizabeth bent over and put her hands on either side of her daughter's face. Anne's skin felt smooth, like silk. How she loved to touch it; the softness brought memories back of Anne's birth, how she could not stop herself from stroking soft, sweet-smelling skin of that miraculous child born after long years of barrenness.

Anne's huge eyes suddenly dimmed as realisation struck her. "Mama…are you not coming too?"

"I cannot, my dear heart." Elizabeth shook her head. "You must dwell with your husband's family now, as is proper. You are a princess! I must return to my duties in Norfolk. I will write to you. I am sure someone will read my letters out; maybe her Grace the Queen will allow you to dictate a letter to me in return."

Anne hung her head, her lower lip trembling. "I-I would rather go home with you, mama. I like my new friends, b-but I love you even more…"

"That cannot happen, Anne. Your destiny is set—and your duty." Elizabeth straightened and let her hands drop from Anne's smooth cheeks, as she struggled to quell the sorrow that sought to overwhelm her.

Anne began to weep quietly, soft gulping sobs. Teardrops jewelled on her long, dark eyelashes.

Elizabeth would not let her daughter down by showing her own intense grief at their parting. "Farewell, my little Nan," she whispered. "May God and the Blessed Virgin watch over you in the days and years to come."

"You must take your medicine, your Grace!" Doctor Caerleon loomed over little Nan's bed like a great black raven in his ebony robes, his broad-brimmed hat sending shadows over his gaunt visage with its break-like nose. In one hand, he held a flagon with foul-smelling steam coiling from its brim.

"I-I do not want any more!" Anne turned her face into the bolster, slow tears tracking down her yellow-white cheeks. Her sprinkling of freckles stood out darkly upon her taut white flesh. "It tastes horrible."

The physician cast a frustrated glance towards Anne's nurse, Joan, who was wringing her hands and strutting nervously around the chamber.

The woman approached her small charge, leaning over and stroking the sweat-soaked hair back from the damp, pallid brow. "Now, your Highness. You must be a good girl and take what Doctor Caerleon offers. He is the Queen's own physician and is great in wisdom; he knows how to make you better."

Anne had been bedridden for over a month. Several of the royal children had fallen ill at the same time but had recovered quickly from whatever malady assailed them. Little Nan, however, had burned with a high fever that grew worse instead of better; she coughed and vomited and felt pain in her belly and all her joints. A rash dappled her small body, red and angry. At first, she had readily let Lewis Caerleon ply her with his medicines, but she now felt so weak and nauseous she could not bear to swallow even the smallest drop of his foul-tasting medicinal brews.

"Is there nought else you can give her?" Joan rounded on Caerleon as Anne, with a piteous moan, hid her face with the sweat-soaked coverlet. "Or some way of sweetening the drought for a child's taste?"

"My potion is not some fancy at a banquet," snapped Doctor Caerleon, his lips drawn in a thin line. "It is a strong medicine containing good Yellow Orpiment and Antimony."

Joan's face crumpled, and she twisted her hands nervously in her voluminous linen apron. "I pray you do not take offence, but it seems to make her worse. These belly pains and retching…."

"Nonsense! What she experiences is almost certainly no more than the evil humours that afflict her being expelled from her body. Such expulsion often makes the patient appear sicklier for a time. I am certain that if her Grace continues the course of her medicine, she will recover."

"But why has she not recovered already? The other royal children have thrown off their ills and are happily playing, while Anne still lies abed."

The physician sighed irritably. "The Princess is both small and slight for her age, which will not help her condition. She has a more delicate constitution."

Joan took little Nan's hand, hot and clammy to the touch. "Come on, my dear lamb, drink the good doctor's potion. Do it for me, your loving nurse, Joanie. For the Queen and for the sweet princesses who love you like a sister. For your mother…"

Anne rolled over, struggling weakly into a sitting position, her back supported by the bolster. "Is mama coming to Placentia? Please say she is, Joanie. I want to see my mama…."

Joan bit her lip. Letters frequently arrived from Kenninghall addressed to Anne, but frequently they were left unopened by Anne's governess or the Queen, and the Dowager Duchess of Norfolk had never visited Greenwich in person. Joan suspected no one had ever invited her, by chance or by design. But surely, she would come, in all haste, if she knew her child was ill. Joan had an uncomfortable feeling in the pit of her belly that no one had informed the Duchess of Anne's illness either. Queen Elizabeth had her own favourites, and Elizabeth Talbot was not one of them. Joan was loyal to Her Highness, but this seemed *wrong*. The girl had a living mother, and she should receive news of her child's wellbeing—or lack of it.

Anne cried out again and slumped on her side in a foetal position, her thin hand fluttering to her stomach. "My belly... It hurts so much, Joanie!"

"And that's why you must heed Doctor Caerleon's advice, my petal," said Joan. "Once you've swallowed it, I will get you some honey to take away the nasty taste."

Anne's face crumpled; a few spots of sweat broke out on her brow. Her mouth moved as if she were about to cry out in protest, but instead she sank down, defeated, her eyes dull. Joan thought those sad eyes looked strange—the pupils so huge the irises were near enough black. The nurse felt the urge to cross herself, but she forced herself to smile.

"Come, I'll help you, Princess." She slid a hand on Anne's back and gently pushed her upright again. Under her palm, through Anne's fine linen nightdress, the child's flesh burned like fire.

"Doctor Caerleon, I do not like what I am see...'"

Ignoring Joan, the physician bent over Anne and pressed his beaker to her lips with some force. "Drink it down, Highness, and soon you will join in merriment with your companions once again."

Anne's lips reluctantly parted, and the potion, sludge-grey mixed with bile-yellow streaks, oozed into her mouth. She choked almost instantly and made to spit it out on the sheets.

"Swallow!" ordered Doctor Caerleon, suddenly fierce and commanding. He grabbed her shoulder, his fingers digging into her flesh.

"You forget yourself, sir!" Joan cried, eyes flashing in anger. "Don't you speak to her like that. Do not *touch* her! She is the wife of a prince, do not forget."

Caerleon ignored Joan and forced the remainder of his elixir into Anne's mouth. When it was all gone, he thrust the flagon into the bag of remedies and instruments he always carried and glared over at Joan. "I have not forgotten my place—it is precisely *because* of her rank that I spoke so harshly and forced medicine into her. How much worse it would be to see the Queen's daughter-by-marriage die through wilful stubbornness!

So hold your tongue, woman, and do not forget *your* place. You are solely here for the menial tasks of dressing, bathing and cossetting highborn children, while I tend to their health and hold their very lives in my hands. My knowledge was learned in the halls of academia at Cambridge and then Oxford—what knowledge of medicine have you, a humble servant?!"

Face crimson, Joan bridled but kept her peace; this was a battle she, coming from humble origins, could not win. "When will you come to tend the Princess again?" she asked in a flat voice.

"When I am needed," said Doctor Caerleon. He hoisted up his heavy bag and strode towards the door, gazing haughtily over his shoulder at Joan. "Now I must go and report back to the Queen."

Joan settled Anne into bed, telling her a long tale from her home village of Woolpit in Suffolk, a story about the mysterious Green Children, a brother and sister, who had arrived there during a summer storm. "All green they were like the grass," said Joan, "and they didn't know English or French or Flemish. They would eat no meat, nor would they take gruel—they ate only broad beans and nought more. Now the people of Woolpit, being good Christian folk, took these strangers in, despite their odd ways, and gradually they learned to speak English. The girl told the villagers they had come from a place called St. Martin's Land, but she could not say where in the world that might be."

Anne tried to show interest, but her voice was thin and hoarse, punctuated by gasps. "What happened to them?"

"Well, they couldn't go home, because no one knew where 'home' was, so a local farmer and his wife adopted them as their own. Slowly, they began to eat normal food and eschew their beans, and as they did so, the green colour vanished from their faces."

"Did they live happily ever after?" Anne's eyes were closed, her lashes falling like spiderwebs on her drained cheeks. Her breathing seemed odd to Joan, too rapid. It reminded her of rabbits that were frightened…or dying. *In, out, in out,* flanks heaving, big eyes full of fear…

"Of course," Joan said with mock cheerfulness, now regretting that she had chosen that particular tale, for the ending was not so joyful. The green boy had sickened and died, while the girl became a hoyden with few manners and even less morals.

"You …don't have to lie…Nurse Joan." Anne said solemnly. "I am not a baby anymore." She rolled onto her side, opening her eyes, which still looked strange, even unfocused, as if she saw sights not of this world. "When my papa died, mama had to tell me, you know. I didn't even cry, though I was just little then."

"Good Duke John," murmured Joan, bowing her head and crossing herself. The hairs on the back of her neck were rising. Deep in her heart, she knew something was terribly wrong, but who was she to make such a judgement, to make a fuss? As Doctor Caerleon said, she was an unlearned menial, hired to dress and wash and clean up dribble…

"D-don't be sad." Anne's eyelids drooped again. "Papa's not sad. He was sick like me…But now he is smiling"

"Smiling?" The corners of Joan's wide mouth dropped down in dismay. "What do you mean, my petal? Your lord father is in heaven with Christ and the saints."

"No." Anne's head made a little side-to-side movement. "He's here…watching me. He's standing behind your shoulder, Joanie…"

"*Ooh!*" Joan leapt from her stool at the bedside, sending it flying across the chamber, and whirled around on her heels, hand pressed to her thundering heart.

No one was there.

Relief flooded the nurse, and embarrassment too, for falling prey to her own superstitiousness. Nonetheless, her unease for Anne continued. The little girl's mind seemed to be wandering, and Joan had seen similar behaviour several times, when someone gravely ill was near to…

Panic gripped her. Bursts of black dotted the edge of her vision and she felt faint. She had to get out of the room, even if only for a brief spell, to calm her frazzled nerves and compose herself.

Lumbering to the door, she shouted down the hallway for her relief, a maid called Ida, who came in when she needed the privy and helped with heavy tasks like lugging in the Princess's wooden bathing tub.

The other woman arrived a few moments later, face pinched with concern. "Is ought wrong, Joan?"

"I need some air, is all," muttered Joan, wiping her forehead with her arm. She felt sweaty and bilious.

On the bed, Anne gave a little moan. "Please don't go, Joanie. I want you to be here with me…just a little longer."

"I'll be back," Joan assured her. "Don't you worry, my dear little Princess. Remember, I said I'd get you some honey to take away the nasty taste of Doctor Caerleon's potions? I clear forgot till this minute. I shall go to the kitchens at once to get it for you…"

Joan stumbled out into the corridor, gasping for air free of the taint of the sickroom, pulling the heavy oak door firmly shut behind her.

In the kitchens, Joan roused one of the cook's young apprentices, who was sleeping on a pallet near the still-warm oven. "Her Highness would like some honey, Ralph. I know it is very late, but…"

The youth nodded sleepily and clambered to his feet, trundling into the nearby larder. He returned with an earthenware honey pot and handed it to Joan. She thanked him and left the kitchens, hurrying up the poorly lit corridors with their leaping shadows.

She was climbing the spiral staircase towards Anne's bedchamber when a terrible, drawn-out scream echoed through the halls. A wail of terror and shock. Her first thought was Anne, but no…*no*…the voice belonged to a full-grown woman, not a child. Footsteps began to thunder overhead as Joan cowered against the bend in the stair, clutching at the cold stone wall with her free hand.

A flurry sounded from the floor below, and all of a sudden Doctor Caerleon, his midnight robes sweeping out like batwings, shoved past her, making her stumble and fall down several stairs, landing hard on her bottom. The honey jar fell and smashed, its sticky contents oozing across the flagstones in the dim light.

Clambering to her feet, breath coming in huge gasps, Joan lunged back up the stairs. The corridor above, empty when she had first sought the kitchen, was now full of palace servants. She saw the chaplain running full-tilt, his cassock flying in the wind of his speed, the torchlight making a silvery halo of his wispy grey hair. Caerleon was nowhere in sight.

Joan tried to run, thrusting onlookers aside, but her head went suddenly dizzy and her breath caught in her lungs. Nonetheless, she staggered on, caught in a waking nightmare, her footsteps heavy and ponderous as if she walked through clay.

As she reached Princess Anne's chamber, she saw the door flung open. Ida was leaning against it, slumping as if her legs would not hold her weight. Her hands were raised to her face, her cap askew, her hair trailing in mousy tendrils over her shoulders. A thin keening slid from the corner of her mouth.

Joan grasped her sleeve, pulling her arm, forcing her to stand. "What is it?" she cried, her voice shrill and strange in her own ears. "What has happened?"

"D-don't look, Joan…don't look," moaned Ida, clawing at Joan's hand as the older woman made to enter the room. The girl's nails cut scratch marks around her wrist. "I called as soon as I realised. Her eyes…t-they rolled back in her head…"

"I must go to her! Get out of my way, you clod!" Joan gasped, and she pulled away from Ida, almost knocking her over, and stumbled into the bedchamber.

Anne lay on the bed, her head drooping to one side. Her lips were blue. The priest knelt at the bedside, chanting prayers. Doctor Caerleon was striding back and forth like a caged beast, his eyes wild and terrible, sweat streaking down a grey face.

Joan rushed to the bed, wringing her hands. She saw that Anne was still breathing, though shallowly, abnormally. A quiet rattle came from her throat with every indrawn breath.

"Oh, what has befallen my poor charge?" Shaking, Joan sank to her knees and clasped her hands, trying to pray, not no words would come into her head.

The priest rose and started to anoint the young girl with consecrated oil, the Unction of God, making a cross on her brow, hands, feet, and back. "Through this holy anointing, may the Lord pardon you whatever sins you have committed," he intoned.

Joan slithered forward and grasped at the hem of Caerleon's robes. "I beg you, give her something that will restore her. She still breathes…Do not let her die!"

Doctor Caerleon snatched his garment from her clawed hands, glaring at the grovelling woman with anger and disdain. "There is nought more to be done. The child was, sadly, of grievously poor constitution and unlikely to ever live to adulthood. I must deliver the unhappy news to her Grace, the Queen."

He stalked from the bedchamber, and Joan, splayed upon the floor with tears streaking her cheeks, watched as the priest, the sacred anointing finished, performed the Viaticum, placing the thin disc of the Host into Anne's slack mouth and pouring a little of the Holy wine after it. It dribbled on her chin; she could no longer swallow. "May the Lord Jesus Christ protect you and lead you to eternal life…"

The priest gazed down at Anne. Her eyes were half-open, gazing heavenward. Her laboured breathing slowed—one gasp, then silence, one more gasp, then nothing more. The priest crossed himself and laid his thumbs gently on her eyelids, closing them forever.

Joan began to keen, joining in with Ida who still clung to the doorway. "She's gone…*gone*, and I did not even get to bring her the honey that I promised."

Winter gripped the manor house of Endhall in the village of Kenninghall. The ground was hard and frosty, the windows and roof tiles patterned with white. Elizabeth was wandering from the pantry to the vaulted larder deep below one of the house's wings, surveying the stores, writing the numbers into a ledger, and calculating whether her supplies would last through the cold months. There were a number of round cheeses wrapped in cloth; they would last for years. Butter was in good supply, and for sweet things she had dried figs and some sticks of cinnamon. Fresh meat was a greater issue, but she did have some mutton, salted beef, pork, and bacon and a goodly supply of salt fish for fast days and Advent. She had access to several fattened pigeons too, which she would save for the Christmas feast, and several tuns of cheap wine—as poor as it might be compared to the fine wines John imported from France when he was alive. Elizabeth's finances were scanty, and the manor even more difficult and expensive to run alone than she had anticipated. She often ran behind on the servants' wages, and a tile had blown off the roof in a windstorm and had, of necessity, been left unmended. Rainwater seeped through into one of the upper chambers, which was now kept empty owing to the dampness. The manor's encircling wall, built more for privacy than defence, also had several cracks in its mortar, and a portion had slumped over in ruin, its foundations weakened by the heavy winter rains.

Still, the fire in the hearth was warm, and she had a roof over her head if not altogether a sound one. Jane, ever loyal, was still with her, although there was talk of her marrying a local knight. Her other servants, what few she could employ, were discreet and hardworking.

Tucking her ledger under her arm, satisfied that the household would survive the winter, Elizabeth climbed out of the dank vastness of the larder and strolled across the empty courtyard, home only to dead leaves that blew in swirls across the cobbles, to enter the door leading into the Great Hall.

The Hall was empty, save for one aged servant, a grey-haired woman called Winifred, who was stoking the fire with a long metal poker. The room's general appearance was dim and tired, the floor-to-ceiling tapestries faded and threadbare, making the woven faces of knights, huntsmen, ladies, and Greek gods and goddesses featureless blobs in the gloom. Elizabeth thought of when she had permitted Eleanor to reside here, safely away from those who might harass her or wish her harm. She sorely wished her sister still lived; both widows could have given each other succour. Since retiring to Easthall, she had gone to Norwich once, on a pilgrimage of sorts, to visit her sister's tomb in the House of the Carmelites. She had lit candles around the chest tomb with its row of carved weepers and whispered to the bones within, "I pray you watch from God's heaven upon your little niece, Anne, and intercede with the Blessed Virgin, for she is in the King's hands, even as you were, and I trust him no more now than then."

A monk had wandered through the nave of the church at that very moment, and Elizabeth had fallen silent and bowed her head, realising that she had spoken words akin to treason. She really had no reason to feel so fearful of Edward and his Queen, not now—and little Nan appeared content enough from the short and irregular missives she received, telling tales about ponies and puppies and new gowns the Queen had made for her.

Wandering over to the large stone fireplace, stained black with ash, its mantle decorated with flower patterns in a style from a hundred years past, she warmed her chilled hands, then beckoned for Winifred to bring her a stool and a pillow. As she sat with the flames at her back, savouring their heat, she said, "Go and fetch Jane for me, Winifred. Ask her to bring my book, the one I recently obtained from a bookseller in Norwich. I would read awhile before supper is served. She can join me here if she so wishes."

The old woman curtseyed to her mistress and hurried from the Great Hall. Minutes later, Jane appeared, a book under one arm and an embroidery basket under the other. "I have brought your book as you wished, my Lady." She handed Elizabeth the leather-bound tome and drew up a stool for herself. "How did the accounting go today? Do you wish for me to go over the figures for you? I should have gone to the larder with you, but…" She suddenly sneezed. "I have some unpleasant malady brought on by the cold weather."

"Do not worry about helping; you rest, my friend," said Elizabeth. "From what I can see, we shall not starve this winter, although our fare will be plainer than in the old days. And, yes, I would gladly have you look for any errors on my part when you feel better. Do not be afraid to tell me if you find them. I am far from perfect in such matters, and of late, it feels as if my head is stuffed full of clouds, making my thought unclear." She glanced at Jane out the side of her eyes. "I doubt that makes much sense to you, though, Jane."

"Oh, madame, it does," Jane replied earnestly. "You have been through so much, and I know you do not hear often enough from little Nan, which I am sure is no fault of the child, but rather her present guardians."

"I am more fortunate than many," said Elizabeth. "I did not mean to complain. And perhaps when Nan gets older, she will send letters she has written herself. Till then, I must try to amuse myself and find solace in other things."

She opened her book on her lap. With all the work of managing her estates, she had not had time to even open the cover yet. Lazily she flicked through the illustrated pages...*Sir Gawain and the Green Knight, Purity, Patience,* and *Pearl.*

The legend of the Green Knight was well-known to most folk as a rousing, heroic tale for mummers to act out at a Christmas banquet. At the moment, it did not hold her interest. She knew the story too well, and it reminded her that there would be no such jolly frivolities at Easthall this Christmas.

She flicked on past *Purity* and *Patience*, but stopped on the first page of *Pearl,* which her old friend Anne Montgomerie had recommended to her. Her heart began to thump in her breast as she started to read the words of the poet.

What had at first seemed like a simple allegory, a pretty work of poetry full of clever, sparkling, alliterative rhymes, took on a new meaning, one highly personal to Elizabeth:

Alas! I lost my Pearl of old!

I pine with heart's pain unforgot;
Down through the arbour grass it rolled,
My own pearl, precious, without spot.

The poem's author was writing about a child, a young daughter he had unexpectedly lost to death. Elizabeth's eyes dampened; the candlelight blurred. She wiped at her face, not wishing Jane to witness her weakness. Time had passed and yet still she could not move on.

"Are you all right, my Lady?" Jane peered at her with concern. "You have worked so hard these past few days. It has taken its toll on you. Marry, the King should have invited you to Eltham for Christmas as mother to his son's bride. But he got what he wanted with the Mowbray inheritance, didn't he? So now he no longer cares a jot about you. I do not know why he…"

"Jane, *Jane*!" interrupted Elizabeth, not wanting to hear repeated the ugly truths that haunted her every day. "This is not a matter I wish to discuss. Do you understand? Rather than gossiping, fetch me a posset from the kitchens. It will soothe me well."

Jane flushed, realising she had spoken far too freely. "My Lady, I shall go at once," she whispered, rising from the stool where she had settled with her embroidery. She gave a quick, awkward curtsey, then fled the Hall, her footsteps quickly fading into the distance.

Elizabeth continued to read the *Pearl* poem, that sorrowful tale of a father's longing for his dead child, in which he lay upon the grassy burial mound that was her grave and bewailed his loss to heaven and earth.

...in that place it slipped from me
I wait, and wish, and sore complain;
Once it would bid my sorrow flee,
And fair fortunes return again;
It wounds my heart so ceaselessly,
And burns my breast with bitter pain.
Yet never so sweet a song may be

As this still hour soothes my brain,
While truth's verity I muse in vain
How clay should her bright beauty clot;
O Earth! a fair gem you do stain,
My own Pearl, precious, without spot!

"I too once had such a pearl," she murmured, her shaking hands tightly gripping her book. "At least, God willing, I shall only know a little sorrow, and never that poet's loss." She sighed and closed her eyes, letting the book drift shut.

As she did, she heard Jane's footsteps again, growing ever louder. She was running. Elizabeth frowned. Why was she in such a hurry? The posset milk would not even have boiled….

Jane skidded through the door into the Great Hall, her gown tangling about her ankles and almost tripping her. She clutched at a motheaten tapestry, almost dragging it down as she struggled to stay upright. Another servant rushed in after her—old Martin, who guarded the gate with his son, Tom. A lantern swung from his grip; the smell of winter clung to his long woollen cloak.

"Jane, what is the meaning of this?" Elizabeth leapt from her seat, still clutching her book. "And you, Master Martin. What on earth has brought you indoors? Is there some sort of trouble?"

"Me lad Tom's outside at the gate, your Grace," said Martin. "As for trouble, well, I cannot say—but there's a rider outside, demanding admission."

"A rider…at this time of the night. On his own?"

"That's why we kept him outside, your Grace. The lateness of the hour set our teeth on edge too. So I thought I should clear his entrance with you before Tom unbars the gate. The rider wasn't too happy 'bout that but…" He shrugged. "The safety of this household is paramount."

"Has he said who he is or who has sent him?" Elizabeth asked. "Has he shown you any cognizance?"

Old Martin looked uncomfortable, stomping from foot to foot. The candlelight glittered on specks of icy rain clinging to his grey beard. "He did show a badge of the *Rose en Soleil*."

Elizabeth's pulse began to race. "That's the King's badge, as you well know! Martin, what has come over you? Why have you not let him in? Have you taken leave of your senses?"

"Anyone can have that badge, madam, even a rogue. Could have stolen one, even killed to get it. It could be a ruse to get into the hall. There are desperate men in these parts, and with it bein' so late and unexpected... I'm not saying the man's a liar, but he could well be."

There was another loud crash, this time in the inner courtyard of the manor house. A man was shouting, his tone full of belligerence, followed by a loud yelp of pain. "Ah, that's my Tom's shout, that is!" yelled Old Martin, dropping his lantern with a clatter.

Jane shrieked as the lantern tipped on its side, the still-lit candle and hot wax streaming towards the worn rugs laid over the rush matting. Jumping up and down like a mad thing, she trod on the flames till they were extinguished—the threat of fire was always a fear in any great home. Martin lunged for the corridor leading to the courtyard, but suddenly he was grabbed and thrown aside, falling into a heap on the flagstones with the wind knocked out of him. A hooded, storm-battered figure stepped over him and stalked into the hall.

"You won't pass me!" growled Old Martin stalwartly, recovering surprisingly quickly for a man his age. He had been a soldier once, fighting at Wakefield many years ago. Teeth gritted, fists raised, he clambered to his feet and shoved himself in front of the cowled stranger.

The man halted, gloved hand out. "I mean no harm to any in this house, far from it. Why do you and your thick-headed assistant not listen to me? I am here bearing a message of import for the mistress of this house, the Dowager Duchess of Norfolk. A message from his Grace, King Edward IV. So let me pass or be damned..." He spat the last words out with an angry snarl and took another stride forward, pushing Martin back against the wall.

Elizabeth was shaking, but angry too. "You seek the mistress of this house, sir? I am she whom you seek. How dare you lay hands on my servants? You say you come from King Edward, yet you act the brute and hide your face. No wonder my men did not wish to admit you. Cast back your hood or leave at once."

The newcomer reached up and pushed back his hood, revealing a thin, white face, weary from a long journey, topped by a cropped bowl of sandy hair. "I am who I say I am, your Grace. Mathew Grene, a courier employed, and much trusted by his Highness the King. I know the hour is late, but I was delayed upon the road by floods and fallen trees, and my news is of great importance and cannot wait till morn." He drew a fold of his mantle aside and gestured to the *Rose en Soleil* badge pinned to his shoulder.

Silver…That was less likely to be a forgery than if it had been wrought of pewter.

But yet Elizabeth was still not certain of the newcomer's intent, so strange and agitated was his manner and his aggression towards her servants. "So, this message is of great importance, yet you come dressed like a vagabond and with none to vouch for you?"

"You have probably not heard, living in this far-flung place," said Grene, with a trace of condescension, "that King Edward has been establishing a system of couriers for a future war with Scotland. Travelling fast is the priority, not niceties in looks or manners. But if you still do not believe I am who I saw, Dowager Duchess, I do not think you can argue with *this*…"

He reached into the scrip bound to his belt and brought forth a parchment scroll. The royal seal blazed red upon it. Kneeling in the first conciliatory gesture he had made since he entered the Hall, he handed it over to Elizabeth.

She stared at the seal. Seals could be forged just like badges, but the design appeared correct and the parchment itself was of excellent quality. And to what end would a forgery be? She guessed Old Martin's initial fear was that the lone messenger had other men hidden in the darkness beyond Endhall's double moat, perhaps with the aim of carrying off a noble widow for a forced marriage. Such outages were known from time to time. But that did not appear to be the case here.

Elizabeth's hands started to tremble. Suddenly, she did not want to know what was written within this scroll. Nonetheless, she slowly untied the red ribbon around it.

The messenger glanced towards Jane, his look stern. "Woman, attend your mistress. She may need you."

Jane blanched and went to Elizabeth's side, visibly upset.

Elizabeth shook her head, perplexed, staring from Jane's worried face to the tired, dour visage of Mathew Grene. "What is this? I am not some old woman in her dotage, so dithery that I must need a maid to hold me up!"

"Duchess." The courier bowed his head; in his black raiment, he almost looked like a mourner at a funeral.

"My Lady…" Jane breathed, her voice a moan. "Oh, my Lady…"

As her apprehension grew, Elizabeth set about breaking the wax seal with numb fingers. The mounted figure of the King cracked and crumbled. Slowly, she unravelled the scroll, holding it up so that the light from the nearby candelabrum illuminated the words written upon it.

She read.

In silence.

And then she let the parchment drop, curling up and rolling as it hit the rush mats strewn across the floor.

She stood like a statue, barely breathing.

"My Lady, please speak. Look at me!" Jane grabbed at her sleeve, shaking her arm.

At length, she stirred. She glanced down at the fallen parchment, the broken crumbs of the wax seal. "I-I have lost my Pearl…" Her hands fluttered up to her throat in a panicked, helpless gesture. "My precious Pearl without a spot."

Jane bit back a cry, understanding instantly. The messenger crossed himself, as did Old Martin, standing beside the door.

Elizabeth took a single step forward, trying to keep her composure and leave the Hall in dignified silence. But a terrible roaring, harsh as a storm at sea, filled her ears, and the chamber grew very bright and then darkened into sparks at the edges of her vision. Knees buckling, she sprawled upon the rushes, nobility rent from her, all hopes torn away, her only child lying cold and dead at far off Greenwich.

"I have lost my Pearl," she whispered once more, and then her head drooped and her eyelids fluttered closed, as Jane flung herself down at her side and screamed to the servants for assistance.

The burial of Anne Mowbray was set for Westminster Abbey. Edward had shown himself generous regarding the interment of his young daughter-in-law; he had ordered three funeral barges to bring her body from the Palace of Placentia and spent a good sum supplying candles and purchasing prayers from high-ranking members of the clergy. He also gave coin, clothes and bread to the customary poor men and children chosen to accompany the coffin to its final resting place, lighting Anne's way to her final resting place with burning brands and lighted tapers.

Elizabeth stood in her harsh mourning black as the funeral cortege entered the vast nave of the abbey and made its way to the chapel of St. Erasmus, recently built on the orders of Elizabeth Woodville, who had planned for her own burial there. The chapel stood within the confines of the abbey's greater Lady Chapel, raised of old by the pious King Henry III and containing coloured Italian tiles and a huge gilded statue of the Virgin and Child in a canopied niche. Tombs of notables rested against the walls, including that of Queen Catherine of Valois, the wife of Henry V.

The King and Queen were not present at little Nan's burial, for it was considered unseemly for the monarch and his consort to stand in the presence of death. Other nobles were there, though— little, black-swathed Margaret Beaufort and her shifty-eyed third husband, Thomas Stanley, and a number of the Queen's sisters, all draped in sombre veils. Anthony Woodville had come on his sister's behalf, to represent her; her firstborn son, Thomas Grey, stood at his side, his handsome, insolent face bland and bored. Lord Hastings had come as a representative of Edward, bringing along his wife, Katherine Neville, who seldom came to court, leaving her husband to his carousing with the King. Others of high title and noble name drifted past: Bourchier, de la Pole, FitzAlan, Beauchamp, Stafford and more. Even the old duchess of Norfolk, Katherine, Anne's great-grandmother, arrived in a litter carried by six strong men in mourning garb. The old lady glared around her fiercely, daring any Woodvilles to approach—at the age of sixty-eight, she had been coerced into taking John Woodville, scarcely more than a lad, as her fourth husband, an abhorrent arrangement designed to give the scrawniest whelp of the Woodville litter a decent income. People had called the union the 'diabolical marriage' and it fuelled the dislike most of the nobility had for the Woodville family.

The funeral hearse glided through the incense smoke leaking from the censers and entered the door to St. Erasmus' chapel. As Anne's kinsman, John Howard had assumed the role of chief mourner, walking in the rear behind the coffin, dressed in solemn black. The hearse was decked with pennants showing emblems of Anne's ancestry: the Arms of Thomas Brotherton, first Earl of Norfolk, the Rampant Lion of Mowbray, as well as the Arms of her husband, Richard of Shrewsbury, impaling her own. A marriage that would never be completed—although the young prince would keep his wife's lands nonetheless.

Elizabeth smiled bitterly beneath her dark veiling. There was every chance that when Prince Richard grew to manhood, he would have no memories at all of the little girl who helped make him wealthy...

The hearse stopped before the high altar in the chapel. Behind the altar, encased in an ornate alabaster frame, was a reredos of the martyrdom of St. Erasmus—a horrible and disturbing sight, showing the saint splayed upon a table with his bowels being drawn out by the turning of a ship's windlass.

Elizabeth averted her eyes from the grisly scene and concentrated on what was more important.

Anne, her daughter, her Pearl, her only child.

She could see her daughter's coffin clearly now as the mourners set it down and bowed, before retreating into the shadows.

Tall sweet-smelling candles ringed the small lead coffin, child-shaped and bearing a metal plaque that read, *Here lieth Anne, Duchess of York, daughter and heir of John, late Duke of*

Norfolk, Earl Marshal, Marshal of England; late the wife of Richard, Duke of York, second son of the most illustrious prince Edward IV, King of England, France, and Lord of Ireland; who died at Greenwich on the 19th day of November. A.D. 1481.

The Bishop of London, his lined old face a creased blur through the smoke coiling from the tall tapers, began to intone the Mass of the Dead, the Requiem. The voices of Westminster Abbey's choir rang out, rising into the soaring vaults high above, echoing between ghostly tombs of ancient kings and pillars of adamant:

> *Requiem aeternam dona eis, Domine.*
> *Et lux perpetua luceat eis.*
> *Te decet hymnus, Deus, in Sion,*
> *Et tibi reddetur votum in Jerusalem*
> *Exaudi orationem meam*
> *Ad te omnis caro veniet.*

> *Kyrie, eleison!*
> *Christe, eleison!*
> *Kyrie, eleison!*

Accompanied by the thunder of the organ, the sound of that dirge washed over Elizabeth in a great, all-consuming wave. She swayed a little, almost overcome, but forced herself to stay upright, her gaze fixed upon Anne's lead coffin. Such a little, meagre coffin... Nan had always been small for her age, and now she would grow no more, a child forever throughout eternity.

As the funeral Mass progressed, Elizabeth began to feel as if it might never end, as if she would stand forever trapped in this dreadful moment of grief and loss and farewell.

But suddenly, a ray of sunlight shot through a window high above, illuminating the dim chapel, streaking over Anne's coffin, missing the grisly image of St. Erasmus, and landing instead upon a stone carving of the Virgin high on the wall.

She, the Christ Child on her knee, shone out all white and gold, a symbol of hope...especially to a mother who had lost her only child.

As swift as it had come, the beam of light faded and the abbey's smoky gloom returned. The Mass was over at last. John Howard motioned to the other mourners who had carried in the hearse. Anne's small coffin was removed from its bier and carefully placed into its prepared resting place, a shallow crypt below the flagstones of the floor.

"My Lady...your Grace?"

Elizabeth woke as if from a dream. Jane was whispering near her ear, trying to rouse her. "All are leaving; it is time to go. Dear sweet Lady Anne is safe in the arms of Christ and his Mother for all eternity."

Nodding dumbly, Elizabeth let her lady-in-waiting guide her away from the chapel as if she were a doddering old crone. Faces blurred around her; she did not want to look at them and see the expressions of pity, of compassion real or feigned—or the boredom she had noted on the visage of Thomas Grey, who was doubtless eager to swagger off to the stews when the abbey emptied out.

Once, she glanced over her shoulder, at the empty hearse and the new grave, soon to have a fitting monument above it, the King's finances willing.

In a whisper, she intoned the words of the *Pie Jesu*, but in English rather than Latin, and with one word of her own insertion:

Merciful Jesus, O Lord, grant my child rest.
Merciful Jesus, O Lord, grant her eternal rest.

After little Nan's death, Elizabeth threw herself into a flurry of activities to help ease the pain of her bereavement. She restored the church tower of Kenninghall and continued to finance work on the new church of the Holy Trinity at Long Melford, a project which she had begun several years before, along with other notable local families, the Cloptons, the Howards, the Cranes, and her old friend, Anne Montgomerie. She visited the site whenever she was able—the church, though still in the early phases of rebuilding, was lofty and of intricate beauty; she planned to make it the fairest in all of Suffolk and to fill its windows with pictorial panels of its patrons, herself included.

When not at Melford, she frequently visited Norwich, enjoying the busyness of its streets and the feel of ongoing *life* that sometimes eluded her in Easthall, where the hours could pass like days in sleepy solitude. While in Norwich, she would visit her sister's grave in Whitefriars and speak to her cold marble tomb as if she still lived. It gave her a certain comfort, believing that perhaps, beyond the circles of the world, Eleanor might hear her…but it saddened her that now, after all these years, she could scarcely remember her sister's face, only that her expressive eyes were rich and dark, much like little Nan's.

On rarer occasions, she journeyed further afield to Cambridge, where, following in Eleanor's footsteps, she had taken up the patronage of Corpus Christi College in a tribute to her lost sister. Dr Thomas Cosyn, Elizabeth's old chaplain, was proctor there, having first been appointed to the fellowship by Eleanor when she had endowed the college. Dr Cosyn, learned and wise with his Degree in Divinity, gave her comfort for her losses, and encouraged her to continue her church-building efforts and other good works pleasing to God.

Returning to Long Melford to examine the latest work on the church, she finally met up with her old friend, Anne

Montgomerie, who was also heavily involved in the building project. They had known each other in the past, but changing fortunes had sundered their friendship in recent years, with Anne moving to Essex after her husband's death. However, they had kept in contact through occasional letters.

The two women met at the local manor owned by John Clopton, chief among those committed to raising the new church as a testament to God's glory. Master Clopton was married to Alice Darcy, Anne's sister. John and Alice had gone on pilgrimage to Canterbury, but in their absence, their children made their aunt and her guest welcome. Elizabeth and Anne embraced, genuinely glad of their renewed acquaintance, before dining privately in the solar, enjoying a light repast of buttered herring kippers followed by an almond-milk tart flavoured with cinnamon, rose petals and violets.

"I am so glad to see you, Anne." Elizabeth looked warmly over at her old companion as the servants took their trenchers and replaced them with a tray of wafers and mazers of hippocras. "Forgive me for my silence in recent years. After John's death, and then my daughter's marriage and…" A shadow flitted across her face.

Anne Montgomerie reached out and laid her hand over Elizabeth's. "You know that I, of all your friends, know best your suffering and at whose hand much of it happened, for I have suffered similar, although, thank God, there was no child involved."

Elizabeth nodded. Anne had been widowed in 1462, when her husband John Montgomerie was beheaded for supposed involvement in a Lancastrian plot to kill King Edward, alongside William Tyrrel, Thomas Tuddenham, John de Vere, Earl of Oxford, and the Earl's son Aubrey. John Tiptoft, the Butcher of England, a learned but remorseless man without an ounce of mercy in him, oversaw their trials. Only by some miracle was John Clopton, master of the manor house of Melford, absolved of guilt and allowed to live.

"Do you ever think of marrying again?" Anne sat back, sipping her hippocras. Evening light danced through the window panes, warm red-gold across the white linen tablecloth. "You are young yet and still, if I might say it, very handsome to look upon."

Elizabeth gave an unladylike snort of laughter. "Truth be told, if some suitor should ardently press his suit, I would seek religious sanctuary. Who would the King permit me to marry, I wonder? Some loathsome creature of his to make sure I kept my mouth firmly closed in regards to Edward and his secrets."

Interested, Anne leaned forward. Elizabeth had never spoken of Eleanor's entanglement with the King to anyone, not even her confessor, but so many tales already swirled through the courts of Europe about Edward of York, the Rose of Rouen—that he was the son of a lowly archer called Blaybourne and hence was a bastard, that his marriage to Elizabeth Woodville was irregular in some unknown manner, though the rumours lacked detail.

"What do you know about our dear King?" said Anne. "I am most intrigued by your comment, Elizabeth." After John Montgomerie's execution, his brother Thomas had wholly espoused the Yorkist cause, and Anne had bent the knee too, for her own sake. But Anne had not forgotten or forgiven; the evidence for John Montgomerie's involvement in the Lancastrian plot was flimsy by anyone's standard.

"I beg you, do not ask me too much. You already know of my servants who were executed on a pretext that they, too, were involved in plots against the Crown. Then came the marriage of my daughter. So many other brides Edward could have chosen for his son, but he wanted the Norfolk inheritance for the boy. However, there is more, much more, though I dare not speak of it."

Anne twisted a corner of her veil thoughtfully. "Hm, if I had to guess… It seems as if the King was making certain you would beno trouble, with your daughter close enough to a hostage in his keeping, as dreadful as that sounds."

"You are not far wrong, Anne. At least that is what I have long believed."

"Christ's Teeth, what a tangled web! As your John is as dead as mine, I will ask it, though you might think me impertinent. Were you once Edward's mistress?"

Elizabeth's cheeks paled. "No, definitely not *that*, I swear to you, Anne. He appeals to me not at all." She gave a slight shudder.

"You have grown white as curds, my friend. Therefore, I shall ask no more. It is clearly too delicate or dangerous a matter to be spoken of." Anne passed her friend the plate of wafers. "But surely you must have some plans for the future if you are not to remarry."

Elizabeth sighed. "Only to continue building, at Long Melford and at Kenninghall. And to live as a good woman in God's eyes."

Anne rubbed her chin. "A noble enough ambition. I have often thought of retiring to a religious house, not to become a nun but to reside among the sisters in my widowhood. Many women of rank retire to convents when their husbands are dead and they have no desire for another marriage. Would you come to stay, if I should ever reside within a convent?"

"I-I do not know, Anne," stammered Elizabeth. "Even though no vows would be taken, I am not sure such a life would suit me. At least not yet."

"It is not a decision to be taken lightly, I agree," said Anne, "but it is always worth keeping one's options open. I, myself, am at present highly engaged with life beyond the cloister walls, but I do think upon the future when my limbs creak with age and money dwindles. I think too of what may happen when the King dies and the regime changes…"

Elizabeth glanced around to make sure none of the servants were in earshot. Encompassing the King's death was treason and punishable by execution, and both women had been under suspicion before. The history of Anne's husband made her position as precarious as Elizabeth's. "Dear friend, do not—the danger…" she murmured.

Anne lifted a hand, gesturing for Elizabeth's silence; she continued as before, although she lowered her voice to a whisper.

"I do not much fear danger or death, Elizabeth. Not anymore. I will have my say, just between me and you, as I know you would never betray my confidences. Tumultuous times lie ahead. I foresee a time of peril and flux that may come sooner rather than later."

Elizabeth shook her head, perplexed. "The King is still but a young man. He will rule for many long years yet."

Anne's brows rose, her mouth pursing. "A man may be young but not in good health. He was the Achilles-like victor of Towton once; now he is merely the victor of the feast, eating so much, I hear, that he purges and then begins his gluttony again. He was once called a giant among men for his height; now he is called that for his great girth."

Despite herself, Elizabeth fought back a guilty giggle. "Oh, Anne, you are too wicked, but I cannot disagree."

"That is not all." Anne pulled her cushioned stool closer to her friend so that she could lower her voice even further. "I've heard tell that he is not well. His face is bloated, not just his belly; they say he is dyspeptic and oftimes breathless. He did not go north to help the Duke of Gloucester in his engagement with the Scots, although he had promised his aid. Hence, other than reclaiming Berwick, little was accomplished."

"I wonder if there is ill feeling with Richard of Gloucester because of Edward's failure," Elizabeth pondered with a frown. In the year after Nan's marriage, Gloucester's wife, her cousin Anne Neville, had written to her, and she had written back in return. However, when her daughter died, the letters ceased. She did not blame her cousin; she knew the Duchess of Gloucester was a doting mother with a frail son who was an only child, even as Nan had been *her* only child. The tragedy of Nan's death doubtless felt too close to home, followed as it was by the death of Mary, one of King Edward's daughters, just as the King was arranging a betrothal to a Danish prince.

Anne shrugged, but then said, "Richard of Gloucester seldom shows his feelings on such matters, but it is true that he comes to London only when expressly summoned ever since the execution of his brother Clarence."

"If the King's health is waning, we must still pray for his renewed strength and power, no matter how we feel about past wrongdoing." Elizabeth grew serious, her eyes shadowed. She twisted a ring on her finger, one John had given her, its bezel inscribed with the name of Mowbray and Talbot. "Remember, his son, the Prince of Wales is still but a boy. Can you imagine if the worst happened? Another child-king on the throne. Every time such has occurred, that King's reign has proved disastrous—and twice brought the monarch in question to an unhappy doom."

Anne nodded. "As it is said, 'Woe to you, O land, when your king is a child'!"

"Of course, the boy would have good counsellors around him, most likely Duke Richard, as he is his closest male relative of royal blood."

"I would not count on that." Anne's eyes narrowed. "I have heard rumours that the *Queen* wants to be Regent should anything happen to the King, with Anthony Woodville, Thomas Grey, and others of her faction as counsellors of state."

"They would never be accepted!" cried Elizabeth, incredulous. "Not by the old blood of England, at any rate."

"When has unpopularity ever stopped the Woodvilles? They would fight tooth and nail, I deem, to remain powerful, moulding their young protegee in ways beneficial to them. Even the King himself has grown weary of them, maybe even weary of *her…*"

"What do you mean?"

"The harlot Shore's wife is uppermost in the King's affections these days. Dame Grey…" she rudely used the Queen's name from her first marriage to the Lancastrian John Grey, "has lost favour. She has even been removed as executor of the King's Will and plans for her own eventual burial not with Edward at Windsor but alone, in St. Erasmus' chapel. So, these days, she is left to her own devices, whatever they might be."

"This is troubling," murmured Elizabeth. "For all that the King may have done in the past, since the time of his second reign, England has enjoyed relative peace. With a child crowned and his family divvying up the country between them, we could find the old hatreds and divisions rising again. Where will it all end?"

"Where, indeed," said Anne wryly.

The women finished their repast in silence, as outside the windows of the manor house, the sky grew red with impending dusk. The earlier afternoon's honeyed light had turned to blood. Hot crimson flowed through the mullioned windows.

"Look," said Anne, pointing, "it is as if the heavens are on fire. How beautiful it is! Shall we go out to the church before night falls?"

Together they left Melford manor house with a couple of brawny young men from the household as escorts, though the little town was a peaceful place that seldom saw trouble, either from locals or from vagabonds passing along the old Roman Road that ran through it. More weavers than tavernkeepers dwelt in Melford.

The church stood out like a heaven-bound ship, the prow of its enormous tower sailing up into the eastern sky. An earlier church had stood on the spot in the reign of Edward the Confessor, but all of that ancient structure had been remodelled or removed. Only the Lady Chapel and sections of the nave had survived the ambitious plans of Elizabeth and the other patrons. Now the enlarged windows stood empty, waiting for skilled glaziers to fill them with panes of painted glass.

Elizabeth and Anne walked down the north aisle, bathed in the ever-deepening scarlet light, as red as the gore on a battlefield. Up above, through an unfinished section of the eastern roof, a star twinkled, faint against a sky growing rapidly purple with approaching dusk. Bats darted between struts and around pinnacles, shadowy wings silhouetted against the fading heavens.

The two widows glanced upward. "That is where the glass shall be fitted." Elizabeth gestured to several window frames. "Made by the finest glassmakers in all England, it shall show the church's patrons gathered around the image of our Lady holding the body of Christ."

Anne reached out in the gloom and squeezed her friend's hand. "For us childless widows, *this* shall be our immortality, our legacy. God did not see fit for us to pass on our blood through living children, so instead we shall pass on beauty to last through all time. In five hundred years and more, they will still look upon us and remember."

King Edward was dead. A sudden illness acquired during a fishing trip with Lord Hastings had defeated the giant warrior, the victor of Towton, Barnet, and Tewkesbury.

The news had reached the east of England and the bells were rung day and night in Kenninghall. Elizabeth prayed for the dead monarch's soul, as was her Christian duty, but not much in the way of true sorrow touched her heart.

And then more unsettling news reached her home, sent to her by Anne Montgomerie, whose brother-in-law Thomas had become a trusted servant of the King. Trouble was afoot. Richard of Gloucester and the Duke of Buckingham had agreed to rendezvous with Anthony Woodville in Northampton, meeting young Edward V as he journeyed down from Ludlow—but something had gone terribly wrong. Woodville, Richard Grey, and others had been arrested, their men dispersed, and Edward V taken under the protection of the Dukes. Talk of a Woodville plot to kill Gloucester ran wild, and Buckingham displayed carts of weapons bearing the Woodville coat of arms which his men found hidden along the road to Stony Stratford, near the Woodvilles' manor at Grafton. Some men sneered and insisted that this tale of treachery was untrue and that the weapons had been stockpiled there when Edward was contemplating war with Scotland. Eleanor thought that was unlikely; the Scots would never make it to the Midlands, let alone further south, and they had made no move to invade any part of England since the Duke of Gloucester brought his army to Edinburgh the prior year.

Whatever the case, upon hearing of the arrests, the Queen had rushed into sanctuary and holed up there with all her worldly goods scattered around her and her daughters and youngest son—Elizabeth's former son-in-law—at her side. Rumour had it that her brother, Edward Woodville, had put out to sea with half the treasury, likely at the command of the Dowager Queen.

"It sounds like the King's passing is every bit as chaotic as Anne imagined it would be," Elizabeth murmured, crumpling up her friend's hastily scrawled missive and burning it in the nearest fire brazier. "Pray God this madness will cease and peace be restored to England."

Preparations went on for the young King's Coronation. Anne wrote again, telling her that young Edward was now safely secured in the Tower and that Buckingham had managed to convince Elizabeth Woodville to allow Richard of Shrewsbury to reside with his brother. *I do not fathom that Duke*, though, she wrote. *A shifty man, he seems. When was he ever such a good friend of Richard of Gloucester ere now? To the best of my knowledge, few have ever called that boastful Stafford boor a friend...*

Elizabeth laughed to herself at Anne's impression of the pompous Harry Buckingham, which tallied with her own. She then pondered whether an invitation to the upcoming Coronation would arrive for her. After all, her daughter had wed the young Prince Richard; that family tie was still there, even if Nan lay cold in her tomb in the chapel of St. Erasmus. Somehow, though, she doubted such an invitation was forthcoming. What on earth had possessed Elizabeth Woodville to behave in such an extraordinary manner and go into hiding? No doubt she was distraught at hearing of her brother and son's arrests, but her behaviour made her seem, well, guilty of *something*.

With a sigh, she thought back on Edward's death—in some parts of the country, his demise had been announced three days before he died. How had such a grave error taken place? Who sent out word that he was deceased while he still breathed? No wonder whispers of 'poison' ran rife in both England and abroad.

Elizabeth shook her head, perturbed, and disposing of Anne's most recent missive, she walked out into the gardens of Endhall. She would not think about those awful rumours, because they brought her own terrible suspicions to the forefront of her mind. How little Nan's marriage contract had given all of her lands to Richard of Shrewsbury if she should die. This stipulation was irregular, barely bordering on legal. How *advantageous* for Edward's family if her daughter should die before the marriage was even consummated...and die she did, of causes unknown.

She shivered, despite the warmth of the day—it was early June, and the sun rode a bank of fluffy white clouds stretch against the blue of the firmament. A bee buzzed by her ear before darting into a nearby flower. The herb gardens smelt rich and fragrant after rain showers in the night—Lady's Mantle, used by alchemists as a potion against elf-shot; Mandrake, also known as Satan's Apple; St. John's Wort to ward off witches; Tansy for cake batter and bad nerves (she had a draught of it prepared for her once a week, mixed with Valerian and Viper's Bugloss). Further on, violets shuddered in the breeze, as richly purple as a king's mantle, their brightness clashing with nearby Marigolds and pink Gillyflowers.

Elizabeth tried to immerse herself in their beauty, the promise of summer and a new King upon the throne, but at her core, the worm turned, gnawing her heart, her innards. The knowledge she possessed, the unspoken truth about Eleanor. That Edward had married her, then committed bigamy. When Eleanor died, he could have admitted his grave sin and remarried Elizabeth Woodville, and all would have been well. But he did not, perhaps from hubris—who would ever challenge him? Or perhaps from slyness—who knew the truth, save his closest confidants and the priest who had wed him and Eleanor? Only Elizabeth, a lone widow, and he had already dealt harshly with her.

She lifted her eyes to the heavens, a low moan leaving her lips. A headache began to pound in her temples; she pulled off her hennin and let her hair fall down, dark and rich, not as auburn as little Nan's but not the midnight hue of Eleanor's either. Somewhere in-between.

She always seemed caught in-between, no matter what she did.

God forgive her, and her conscience laden with forbidden knowledge. Knowledge she had never imparted even in the confessional. Knowledge that the King's marriage to Elizabeth Woodville had been invalid, which meant his children were bastards.

A bastard would sit upon the throne of England by Midsummer.

Bastard slips shall not take root…

Elizabeth was woken by Jane calling her name, "My Lady, my Lady."

Groggily she sat up, blinking in the strong sunlight that strayed through the shutters in her bedchamber. She scrambled to her feet. "Jane, what is it? Is something wrong?"

"Madam, I journeyed to Kenninghall village this morning." Jane moved to her mistress and helped her into a heavy robe. "The place was abuzz with the latest news from London."

"Oh, and what news is that?" Elizabeth laved her face in a bowl of rosewater handed to her by Jane. The cool splash brought her to full wakefulness…and she was aware her fingers were trembling. "Can it get any more distressing?"

Jane's mouth worked, and Elizabeth realised her maid had the look of a frightened deer, ready to bolt.

"*What is it*?" she repeated. "Tell me."

"Lord Hastings…" began Jane, and then she shook her head in a jerky, uncoordinated motion.

"What of the old goat? He's not causing trouble, is he?"

"My Lady…he is *dead*!"

"Dead!" Elizabeth stared at her maid, shocked.

"Yes, my Lady, executed for treason. 'Tis said he was dragged to a log and beheaded unshriven, though that may be nought more than gossips' exaggeration. But he is most assuredly dead. London is in an uproar."

"But who had the authority to do such an act? Not the young King, surely; he is youthful and untried, and uncrowned as yet. And Lord Hastings was his father's closest friend…"

Jane shook her head again. She seemed to have been struck dumb.

"Jane!" Elizabeth's voice snapped like a whip in nervous frustration. "Speak!"

Jane took a deep gulp of air. "It…it was the Lord Protector of the Realm, madam. Richard of Gloucester."

Elizabeth crossed the room and sank into the window seat. The morning sun reached through the age-bubbled glass, heating her back. "Jesu help us, but why?"

"It is said Hastings had devised some plot with Elizabeth Woodville."

"But Will Hastings was never a friend of the Woodvilles! Recently he and Anthony Woodville came close to blows."

"Even so. But there was a fractious council meeting, and he, along with Lord Stanley and Bishop Morton, were arrested. They were accused of wanting to destroy the old blood of England, in particular the Lord Protector and the Duke of Buckingham. Hastings even brought weapons into the council chamber…"

Elizabeth's hand fluttered to her throat. "I do not know what to make of these tidings, Jane. Never have I heard of such happenings in all my days. What of the young King? Where is he in all this?"

"Safely in the Tower, thank God. He and his brother have been seen practising archery on the lawns. The Dowager Queen is still in sanctuary, which must bring worry to her sons, but no doubt she will come round in time."

"With her brother Anthony still imprisoned? What is happening with that?"

Jane frowned. "The Lord Protector wants him and his co-conspirators held. Indeed, he wants to charge them all with treason against his person, but other council members disagreed with his position, so for the moment all of them are incarcerated in various northern castles."

"Treason!" Elizabeth's eyes widened. "If they should be found guilty…" Her voice trailed away.

"Yes," nodded Jane. "Exactly so."

"Elizabeth, I rode here as fast as I could." Anne Montgomerie stood in the solar at Easthall, gloved and wearing a modest headdress and long, dark travelling cloak.

Outside in the courtyard of the manor, her entourage was dismounting their horses, while Elizabeth's steward and two stable grooms saw to their comfort. The yard was full of noise—animals stamping and whinnying, the jingle of horse harnesses, a groom whistling, the new arrivals laughing. Elizabeth was reminded poignantly of how life had been when John was alive—those heady days when great lords and their entourages would ride up to Framlingham Castle, stay for sumptuous banquets and hunt in the forested grounds beyond the moat. Days when it felt like they lived in fabled Camelot.

Anne was divesting herself of her cloak; Jane carried it away, and Elizabeth dismissed the maid with a brief nod. "You may go for the rest of the day, Jane. I would speak with Lady Anne alone."

As soon as Jane had exited the chamber, Anne strode to Elizabeth and impulsively clasped her hands. "I hope I am the first here," she said breathlessly. "The first to bring tidings of events in London."

"What has happened now? The last I heard was of Baron Hastings' death."

"Much has transpired since that day," said Anne, "and I am glad I am first to tell you…because it involves your family."

"My family?" asked Elizabeth, confused. "Do you mean my brother, Humphrey? Or perhaps my cousin Gilbert?"

"No, Elizabeth." Anne's lips drew into a thin, tense line. "Eleanor…your sister Eleanor."

Blood rushed to Elizabeth's head; blackness pushed at the edges of her eyes. She stumbled and Anne caught her, placing a comforting arm around her shoulders and guiding her to the window seat. As Elizabeth lay slumped in the embrasure, breathing harsh and raspy, her friend hurried to the table in the corner and poured a mazer of wine from a silver ewer. Hastily, she brought the cup over and pressed it to Elizabeth's lips. "Drink," she said, "it will steady you. Take deep breaths and do not try to stand up till you are ready."

"So Eleanor's secret is out. The secret marriage to King Edward." Elizabeth took a deep breath. After her initial shock, she now felt oddly relieved. Unburdened at last.

"Yes." Anne sat beside her in the window seat. "Bishop Stillington told Gloucester that he performed the marriage himself in one of Eleanor's manors in Warwickshire. Ralph Shaa gave a thunderous speech at St. Paul's Cross about 'bastard slips' and now everything has changed. The three estates have debated these revelations and decided that Edward's children are to be removed from the line of succession."

"So, England without a king as it was for the Israelites -*For the children of Israel shall live many days without king, without prince, without sacrifice…*"

"There *will* be a King," said Anne firmly.

"Who? Not Clarence's boy, another child-king to lead us to disharmony! Besides that, he lies under his sire's attainder and cannot inherit."

Anne gave her friend a look as if she thought her witless and moon-mazed. "King Edward has a brother. Next month, the Archbishop of Canterbury will crown King Richard, Third of that Name."

Almost in a daze, Elizabeth sat in the Banqueting Hall of Westminster at King Richard's Coronation feast. Since she arrived, she had been treated as if she were still the Duchess of Norfolk rather than a mere dowager and she was robed and jewelled as such. When she had reached London several days ago, her cousin Anne—now her Grace the Queen—had summoned her into her presence in the Tower, embracing her fondly. "Oh, my dear kinswoman." Anne the Queen's smile had glowed as bright as sunlight. "It has been far too long. Did you ever think you would see this day?"

Elizabeth had smiled wryly and made no answer, for there was none she could make that would be adequate. Then a hush fell as the King himself entered the solar, clad in a long robe of royal blue lined with ermine, adorned with golden pineapples and fleur-de-lys. The robe's hue made his eyes look a vivid blueish-grey in his pale, solemn face.

"Your Grace," murmured Elizabeth, dropping into a low curtsey with her head bowed.

"Rise…rise," said Richard, his voice warm, and Elizabeth immediately did his bidding. For the hundredth time, she wondered if he had known about Eleanor and his deceased brother before the events of the summer, but she decided it did not matter either way. Both Eleanor and Edward were dead and Edward's children disinherited—now was here and the past was gone, if not quite forgotten. It was time to move forward; the old regime was over and done, for good or for ill.

"It does us honour for you to attend our Coronation, Duchess Elizabeth," said the new King. "As my dear kinswoman through marriage, I will see that you are well-treated from this day forward. I heard that you have been involved in the building of a fine church in Suffolk; one day, maybe I shall visit. My family has connections to the town of Clare, not so far away."

"You are kind, your Grace," she murmured.

"I fear you and yours have suffered unnecessarily over the years. It will not continue. The Norfolk inheritance shall no longer be held by my illegitimate nephew, Richard, but granted to the original inheritors who should have taken possession upon your daughter Anne's sad demise—Lord John Howard and the heirs of his body. To you, I shall give a grant for life of the tenements, messuages and lands at Chelsea Hythe, here in London." He smiled. "You may hold them for the service of a single red rose presented on Midsummer's Eve."

Then King Richard beckoned to his Queen that it was time to leave, and together they disappeared into the depths of the Tower, leaving a stunned Elizabeth in their wake.

"Oh, my Lady." Jane, who had been humbly lurking in the background during the royal encounter, rushed up to Elizabeth, hands clasped and eyes brimming with joy. "You'll have no more worries now, for money or for anything else. I can feel it in my bones!"

"Hush, my dear Jane," Elizabeth had told her, taking her hands in her own. "Let us not tempt the capricious fates."

And now she was seated in a place of honour, with the spectacle of the Coronation feast playing out before her. First, John Howard had ridden into Westminster Hall on a charger draped in cloth of gold to drive out gawkers and onlookers without invitations. A high table was erected on the dais with long tables for the guests down the sides of the hall—one for bishops, one for the dukes and earls, one for barons, and one for noble ladies. A young page in a tabard embroidered with a white boar had led Elizabeth to her place among the noblewomen.

A herald blew upon a trumpet, signalling the arrival of the first course. Streams of servers filed into Westminster Hall, carrying platters full of amazing delicacies—venison frumenty in Tuscan broth; pheasant with its tail feathers displayed; roast cygnet, heron, and crane; plump capons amidst lemons; a huge pike stewed in bittersweet sauce; jelly cut into slices; and a huge range of simmering custards and tarts.

Elizabeth ate sparingly, as was her wont, although she tried a small portion of each dish. Long years had passed since last she dined in such opulence, with musicians playing in the gallery and candles burning in the hundreds, and the lords and ladies of the land clustered around, glowing like brightly plumaged birds in their raiment of silk, taffeta, samite, velvet and their jewel-encrusted collars, girdles and necklaces. Emeralds winked like green cat's eyes in the candle-lit hall, alongside rubies like dollops of frozen blood, while white rock crystal burned with icy fire, and sapphires spoke of endless summer skies in lands less cloudy than England.

Looking up towards the dais, she saw the King in his fur-lined Coronation robes eating from a plate of pure gold. Next to him, her cousin Anne, her reddish-blonde hair flowing free over her shoulders, delicately picked morsels from one that was gilt. Richard's good friend, Francis Lovell, stood under the royals' canopy, assuming the role of chief Butler…and then there was Harry Stafford, Duke of Buckingham, in purple just a shade too close to 'royal' than was perhaps appropriate. A tall hat with peacock feathers sat on his curling hair, while around his thick neck hung a livery collar burning with jewelled Stafford Knots depended by an enamelled swan gorged in gold.

Thomas Howard's wife, Bess Tilney, whom Elizabeth knew quite well from her ties to the Howards through marriage, leaned over to whisper in her ear, "Look at Buckingham's face. Cat who's got the cream and yet never satisfied, I hear. My father-in-law should have overseen the Coronation as Earl Marshall and High Steward, but no, Buckingham insisted he should have the honour since he helped the King attain the throne."

"And his Grace the King gave in to him," murmured Elizabeth, watching Buckingham closely. For all the honours granted him, even now he wore a vaguely disaffected look, a sullen poutiness about his mouth.

"I am surprised he even allowed John to carry the crown," Bess Tilney continued, her eyes narrowed. "If his hands hadn't been full of the King's train, I swear he would have fussed till he had hold of the crown too. I am surprised he didn't insist on wearing it on his own head before handing it over for the crowning ceremony," She tittered in a spiteful way. "I think he will bring no good to anyone, Elizabeth. No one can endure him save the King, and I wonder how long that will last. I have heard Richard tires of him already; he promised Buckingham the Bohun lands, but it must go before Parliament first, and Stafford is not best pleased that he must wait."

Elizabeth's attention was drawn away from Harry Stafford as the trumpets blared again. The second course was being carried in by the servers—peacocks still wearing their shimmering plumage, roe deer, partridges in mustard, carp in peppered sauce, followed by both sweet and savoury tarts and coloured and shaped jellies that wobbled in the candlelight.

One of the jellies was shaped like a castle with tall pointed turrets glittering with sugar paste. The walls were pink with rose petals mixed into the jelly, and a little poppet wearing a crown leaned out of one of the windows.

Little Nan would have enjoyed this so! The thought flashed through her mind, making her smile, but then came the usual stab of regret, of grief, the hollow ache that afflicted both heart and stomach. She pushed her trencher away, appetite suddenly quelled.

The Coronation feast continued, but it ran overtime since the new King and Queen were both busy conversing with bishops and nobles who approached the dais. Before long, darkness was falling, and there were torches lit about the great chamber to augment the thin candlelight.

The planned third course of the feast was never served owing to the lateness of the hour. At least the poor folk of London would dine sumptuously that night—the servers would be permitted to take their fill, while the rest of the food would be distributed among the beggars and other unfortunates clustered at the palace gates.

The King, beginning to look weary, motioned that he and Queen Anne would remove to their chambers for the night. They rose beneath their canopy of estate, and the courtiers swarmed around them like bees, Buckingham foremost among them, the Duke's loud laughter drowning out all other voices.

Once the monarchs had departed, clarions ringing out to announce their leave-taking, the rest of the invited celebrants began to file out into the night. Elizabeth said farewell to the other noblewomen on her table and, throwing her cloak around her shoulders, she hurried to the courtyard to find Jane and the chariot arranged to bear her to her lodgings.

Setting off at a good pace through the London streets, she leaned against the backboard of the carriage seat, while Jane, seated opposite, chattered on incessantly about the wonders she had witnessed that day—the silks, the furs, the shoes with golden buckles, and about the lavish food she had devoured and the fine hippocras and malmsey she had imbibed.

Elizabeth smiled and nodded, but her mind was elsewhere; she had taken her fill of splendour. Suddenly, a breath of wind wafted the curtain over the carriage's window aside. Outside, loomed the Tower of London on its hill, with Bishop Gundulf's great keep a ghostly head leering into the gloom. Birds off the river swirled around the turrets, their cries high and eerie, their wings spectral blue in the light of a crescent moon. A single light blazed in one window, a raging eye piercing into the night.

With a jolt, Elizabeth thought about little Richard of Shrewsbury, a prince no more, sitting locked within those stern walls. Was he fearful? Did he understand what had happened? Did he call out for his mother, as Nan had doubtless done when she was not present?

She drew her cloak more tightly around her shoulders. The wind was blowing in off the Thames, cooling the warmth of the summer's night.

As the carriage clattered on, bumping over the begrimed cobblestones, she wondered what would become of the boy, her son-by-marriage if only briefly, and his brother, a king never crowned.

She sighed fitfully and turned her face into the shadows.

The Wheel of Fate had spun again.

Elizabeth sat on a stool in the bedchamber at Easthall, warming her legs beside the fire. "I grow old," she muttered, rubbing at her knee and ankle joints, all swollen and sore. "I need poultices to ease these aches or some rue and willow bark boiled in vinegar to drink."

Stiffly, she moved to a small glass mirror, imported from Italy, which had a gilded frame shaped like two entwined mermaids. Gazing into the glass, she saw a pale face, thin lines fanning out from the eyes and running parallel to her mouth. Her hair, loose in the privacy of her bedroom, was flecked with grey, the silver strands stark amidst the shadows of her tresses.

"I once plucked these hairs of age," she murmured, twisting a curl around a thin finger, "but now, if I did so, I would end up as bald as an egg."

She sighed as she sat on her stool again and watched a spider spin a web on the ceiling high above. She'd find a servant to get the creature down later. She was not afraid of spiders like some women, but watching the creature weave its web, she was reminded all too clearly of the tangled webs woven by men. Webs that could ensnare and lead to tragedy.

King Richard's reign had been short and filled with tragedy. Richard took the crown, seeking to give stability to England, but it became a vicious and deadly burden. His little son Edward had died unexpectedly, sending the King and Queen nearly mad with grief. A year later, Anne followed her boy to the grave, riddled with a consumptive illness so grave that the court physicians barred the King from her bed in her last months. That caused wicked tongues to wag, as they had about the fate of Edward's sons, who had vanished from the Tower, their fates unknown. Many men thought Richard had killed them, but he was silent on the matter, not deigning to make replies to such accusations, while others whispered that the murderer was Harry Stafford, who had rebelled for reasons unknown against his sovereign and paid the price on a scaffold in Salisbury marketplace. He had begged for Richard to see him, insisting he had urgent news he must hear, but the King refused, and Stafford's secrets died on the block.

Then, in 1485, Henry Tudor, the only son of iron-willed Margaret Beaufort, came sailing from Brittany with a rag-tag band of supporters, disaffected Yorkists, many with older Lancastrian allegiances, some Welshmen drawn to his Dragon banner, and scores of foreign mercenaries, including the rabble released from French gaols. He marched from Wales, declaring himself the true King—audaciously, for he had no real claim to the throne at all. Richard led his army to Redemore Plain; he should have won that day, for the Tudor was no skilled warrior, but ill-luck cursed him once again, and his mount floundered in the boggy soil of the plain. Richard was unhorsed and slain fighting in the thickest press of his enemies.

One of Elizabeth's nephews had fought for Richard, another for Henry Tudor, but she would not condemn either man for his choice. She had little to do with her family now, or with the affairs of great men. A new era had arrived but she still belonged to the old.

The new King Henry she had not met, although she had some dealings with his Margaret Beaufort, who now went by the name of 'The King's Mother'. Margaret convinced her to give up the manor of Chelsea Hythe, which Richard had allowed her to tenant for the payment of one red rose. Elizabeth was too weary to fight against Margaret's wants, a fight she would never win anyway, and as she used the manor seldom, she had agreed.

She wondered what Henry was like; from what she'd heard, he was shrewd and secretive, rather like his mother, whom he resembled. Edward's daughter, Elizabeth of York, had married him, a strategic move for the fledgling king which had pleased those whose sympathies still leaned towards the Yorkists. Henry and Elizabeth had already produced a healthy son in 1486, whom they named Arthur as a tribute to that ancient king known for his chivalry.

But even though some spoke of stability, troubles still had brewed in England after Henry claimed the throne by Right of Conquest. Many were not so enamoured of Tudor; Richard's friend, Lord Lovell, led a force from Ireland and tried to oust Henry in favour of a youth who was variously said to be Edward V, alive, Edward of Warwick (who Henry had locked in the Tower) or even a bastard son of Richard's.

Henry Tudor was born beneath a lucky star, unlike his predecessor, it seemed, and his army prevailed in the field yet again, with Richard's nephew, John de la Pole falling in battle, and the boy, whoever he was, taken captive. Henry kept him as a spit-turn in the kitchens, not as merciful and magnanimous a move as it might seem, for it was back-breaking work and hot as the furnaces of hell, and the lads who turned the spit were frequently burnt by the boiling fat. The child was said to be one Lambert Simnel, an imposter from Oxford, but Elizabeth had her doubts. A lad named after an Easter *cake* and an ancient saint who fought for the sanctity of marriage? Unlikely.

Joints still burning, she pushed herself upright. She would go down to Kenninghall church today, to examine the work her masons had done on the Tower. She wanted to pray to…to pray for answers as to what might prove best for her in whatever remained of her life, short or long. Over the last few years, she had begun to feel that Easthall was too remote; as she grew older, she had begun, much to her surprise, to wish for the companionship of other women like herself, especially now that Jane had married and was no longer in her service. She missed her lady-in-waiting, whom she also called 'friend', but Jane's departure had been inevitable once she fell with child, and Elizabeth could do nought but wish her well.

Calling for Alicia, a new girl from the village who had come to attend to her personal needs, she was soon presentably dressed in a dark maroon gown, the gauze veil of her butterfly headdress, a little ragged and a little out-of-date, fluttering over her shoulders.

"Today you shall accompany me to St. Mary's, Alicia," said Elizabeth. "Get a few of the men to accompany us for propriety."

"Shall I call for horses?" asked the girl, a slip of a creature, barely sixteen. She had auburn hair that looked almost purple in the shadows; its hue reminded Elizabeth a little of Nan's, although Alicia's hair was straight as a pin whereas her daughter's had curled, as thick as a horse's mane.

"No, I thought we should walk today," she replied. "The wind is chilly, but I think it might blow the cobwebs from my mind."

The young girl looked slightly dismayed at the thought of a journey in the cold but bobbed a respectful curtsey nonetheless. "May I fetch my cloak and gloves, madam?"

"Of course, but do not tarry. I have spent too long before the fire this morn, and there are tasks to complete before the day is done."

Elizabeth set forth from Eastwell with Alicia trudging dutifully at her heels. The rest of her party followed, unobtrusive but ready to step in should trouble arise. Not that it was likely in a place such as Kenninghall. Still, many were on their guard after the Battle of Stoke Field the year before, just in case any German or Irish mercenaries had escaped the slaughter and were prowling around in English woodlands. "They are likely all cannibals by now!" Elizabeth remembered Old Martin saying in all seriousness, as he made sure the manor house's gates were in good repair. "They can't get home, but with their funny looks and tongues, they can't fit in among normal folks either...so dead bodies for dinner it is."

The church rose up before her, pinnacles wreathed by a thin haze. She glanced at the tower with a smile—the Talbot and Mowbray Arms shone out as a thin streak of sunlight passed over them. The bottom of the tower, too, had adornments she had added, looping patterns that wove together. She had once conferred with Eleanor about their design, so long ago that it almost seemed in another lifetime.

Leaving her attendants outside among the tombs in the churchyard, Elizabeth entered the Norman church door, guarded by a stone dragon and an unusual carving of a riderless though bridled horse, and walked down the south aisle with Alicia.

The church was stately and wide, with light flowing through the large windows she had put in. Eleanor had her hand in that too; one of the windows had been glazed on her orders while Elizabeth was in Burgundy. She suspected Eleanor would have added coloured glass depicting some holy scene or even a commemoration of her family, but she had died too suddenly, and her plan was never completed.

Elizabeth passed a battered chest tomb of some unknown long-deceased knight and entered the Lady Chapel with its soft wall paintings of the Assumption, heavily washed with red that veered towards pink or ochre, and a roof of painted golden stars. A statue of the Virgin awaited, arms outstretched, robes the colour of a clear sky falling back to reveal dazzling white garb beneath. She smiled serenely, benevolent and kind.

Blessed Lady, grant me some of your serenity, your gracious mercy, thought Elizabeth as she went down on her knees. She grasped her amber prayer beads, letting them slide through her fingers like frozen honey or sunbeams. At her side, Alicia plumped down rather awkwardly, her shoes making a loud scraping on the ornamental floor tiles bearing the Mowbray lions. "Sorry," she muttered, remembering to add, "your Grace' only after a long pause.

Elizabeth paid Alicia no heed. The girl was gauche; she was no Jane to keep her merry, but soon, maybe, it would not matter one way or the other. The child would learn as children often did, and there would be less sullen pouting and perhaps more artifice perhaps, for such was the way of the fallen world of men.

The day passed; Elizabeth lost all track of time, knowing only that the sunlight cutting across the windows had deepened in hue. Her prayer was so intense that she felt as if she were floating, rising up, up towards heaven itself. Light spilled into her eyes; she raised them upwards and was dazzled by the beams falling through the Lady Chapel's windows, lighting the golden crown upon the Virgin's head and igniting dust motes whirling in the air.

She gasped, for Our Lady appeared to stretch a hand in her direction, and Elizabeth wondered if she had gone mad or if she was indeed so blessed that she had been sent a heavenly vision, one to guide her on the right path, as visions often guided the mystics and holy anchorites of old.

And then she saw, as a gasp broke from her lips, a small, wispy figure skipping across the tiles, light as a feather, wreathed in the unearthly glow that flooded the chapel. A child, laughing, her voice a faraway echo through time, dancing towards the outstretched arms of the Virgin. Her face was hazy, radiating light, and her hair burning with a deep red flame…

Elizabeth crumpled forward, her own hand reaching out. *My Pearl, I have found my Pearl…at last…*

As quick as it came, the glamour was lifted, the spell shattered. A passing cloud obscured the window high above. The light failed, the dust motes drifting down like dead moths. The Virgin's face was but stone and paint, with a fleck chipped off one cheekbone. The phantom child was gone, and it was only Alicia tugging on her arm, her red hair illumined by the flames of the votive candles set about the space.

"Are you all right, my Lady?" Alicia queried. "I did not want to disturb you at your prayers…but then you had a funny turn."

"I am fine, perfectly fine." Elizabeth pushed the girl's hand away and got to her feet unaided. "But I have made a decision today, Alicia. When I return to Easthall, I bid you summon a clerk to my solar. I have a letter to write to my old friend, Anne Montgomerie, who lives with the nuns of St. Clare in London."

The Abbey of the Minoresses was the largest convent in London. Elizabeth had moved into the Great House at the convent's heart, where noble ladies retired, not as sisters of the order but as gently-born tenants requiring peace and solitude. Anne Montgomerie resided there too, and half a dozen other ladies, all of whom had suffered much in their lives through war and death.

One was kin by marriage, Jane, widow of her brother, Humphrey Talbot, who had died while on pilgrimage to St. Catherine's Mount in Egypt, that holy place where God had appeared to Moses within the Burning Bush. Another tenant was Elizabeth Brackenbury, a daughter of Sir Robert Brackenbury, the Constable of the Tower during Richard's brief reign, who had died fighting beside his liege lord on Bosworth Field. Mary Tyrrell dwelt there too, a niece of Anne's. Mary's brother, James, had gone to the block mere weeks ago, accused of treason—and also of slaying Edward V and Richard of Shrewsbury on the orders of Richard III. It was a spurious accusation, though no one dared protest against it. Tyrrell had served Henry well enough since Bosworth, and if he were truly a regicide, why was the charge brought against him only for the lesser crime of having dealings with the de la Pole family? At one time, King Henry had granted Tyrrell two pardons for unspecified offences—Elizabeth thought that made him look every bit as guilty as those he claimed had murdered the young boys.

She sighed to herself as she strolled around the precincts of the convent with Jane Talbot. Like most others, she wondered what had happened to the princes—to her own son-in-law, the younger of the two boys. Not so many years back, a pretender had come from across the sea, calling himself Richard of England, the lost second son of Edward IV. He had been handsome, tall, and well-versed in courtly manners. Many of the crowned heads of Europe supported his claim. The King had taken him prisoner and had him tortured, breaking his face until he was nigh unrecognisable. Under such duress, he confessed to being an imposter named Perkin Warbeck and was executed…but was there a chance that he truly was who he claimed? She had not seen this 'Perkin', nor would she have recognised him even if he was Prince Richard. Too many years had gone by; her memories had faded, drifting away like leaves in a gale.

Elizabeth was in her fifties now, and of late it seemed death loomed at everyone's shoulder, from the great to the lowly. A year ago, King Henry's heir, Arthur, had married the Spanish Infanta, Katherine of Aragon, to great rejoicing. However, this past spring the promising young prince died of the Sweat at Ludlow, his demise a dagger in his father's heart, Henry's hopes and ambitions wafted away on the miasma of disease. He had another son, Henry, but none spoke of him in the way they had Arthur, nor had he been trained from birth to assume a king's mantle.

Elizabeth spoke of this as she walked with Jane Talbot through the nuns' garden, blooming with flowers that blotted out the pungent odours of London—foetid Thames water, cooking, woodsmoke, animal dung, and the ever-lingering reek of the rotted heads on London Bridge when the wind blew the wrong way.

Before the women towered the abbey church, bearing a spectacular lantern-tower and long cloisters extending to the north. On one side was the postern gate, guarded by a ditch and adjoining the town walls; if one wished, they could stand atop those walls and view the House of the Crutched Friars…and the scaffold on Tower Hill.

Misery and death were not sights she welcomed, and Elizabeth had never even glanced towards that place of execution, not even the day they brought Perkin Warbeck there. In her cosy chamber, she had heard the crowds roar and shriek, though, driven to frenzy by the most animalistic of passions.

"Do you think the King fares well…after Arthur?" She plucked the head off a large white daisy; its petals broke apart, fluttering in the wind.

"Well," said Jane, a short, stout woman with a plain, honest face, "he does have a second son, the Lord Henry…and he has got the Queen with child again, God be praised. Hopefully, the babe will be another boy to ensure the safety of the succession. The King is always fearful that others might still put forth a claim."

"The de la Poles. Henry has already imprisoned William de la Pole in the Tower, after his two brothers fled England for safety. I do not understand the charges against William; he stayed behind when the others disappeared, which surely points to his innocence."

"The King is taking no chances. 'Tis said he has always been deeply fearful of those who might dispute his right to sit upon the throne."

Elizabeth nodded. "He claimed England by right of conquest, but tried to convince many that he had blood-right as well. But all honest men know his claim was weak and that the Beauforts were of bastard line."

"He is also taking no chances with showing the world how far the House of Tudor has risen. He has begun building a tomb in Westminster Abbey, the greatest, most lavish tomb made by any king of England thus far."

"I heard tell of this monument. An Italian will sculpt it, I believe. It seems death is on Henry's mind, whether a new child is on the way or not."

"Henry's health is poor. His eyesight fails—he spends much on useless cures—and his teeth are reported to be black and loose. He hates the spring; he coughs every year till he is sick. He never seemed terribly strong to me. Remember, he did not fight in the battles he won; he watched those loyal to him win the prize for him."

"So he may think the hourglass runs out," Elizabeth said thoughtfully. "We should not be talking about this, though, sister."

"No, but what is left to us but gossip?" Jane gave a little shrug. "And who is there to hear us—the flowers?" She batted at a lavender bush with her hand, dislodging some bees from the purple flowers. "What other pastimes have we, save prayer?"

"We have servants and cooks; we have our pet dogs. We are not nuns!" laughed Elizabeth. "But one thing puzzles me about Henry's grand plan—where will he place this mighty tomb and all its finery? The Abbey is already brimming with tombs."

Jane's gaze slid to the ground. "I do not know. It is said that he plans to remove certain features near the Lady Chapel. Ones he dislikes and does not approve of."

A cold stab of fear pierced Elizabeth's heart; she felt her throat tighten painfully. Surely, *surely*, the King would not touch Anne's tomb in St. Erasmus' chapel? Her daughter had lain there for over twenty years in peace. It would be ungodly and a disgrace to move the resting dead. While saints and kings were sometimes disinterred and borne to new churches, that was often done as a sign of respect, to place them in a finer tomb, one more worthy of their stature or where they might easily be venerated. This was *different.*

"Oh, Jane, this fills my heart with foreboding," she murmured. "Do you think my Anne's grave…" She trailed off, unable to say the unspeakable.

Jane shook her head. "I truly do not know, Elizabeth."

"I must find out. There must be a way!"

A cloud skidded over the sun, plunging the gardens into gloom. Elizabeth lifted her skirts and hurried back to her quarters in the big house within the close, leaving Jane staring at her departing back. Elizabeth did not weep, but inside she was screaming.

She went to Westminster Abbey with Anne Montgomerie. In recent years, Anne had become a leader to the little group of noblewomen living in the house at the centre of the Abbey of St. Clare and St. Francis. She was pious and well thought of by the nuns, but she kept a very firm foot in the outside world as well.

"Abbot Islip is known to me," she told Elizabeth as they made their way through the busy London streets. "He is on friendly terms with King Henry and has dined with him on many occasions, discussing his Highness' plans for the abbey. And feeding the King marrowbone pudding!"

"Marrowbone pudding?"

"The King's favourite, apparently."

"So there is something sweet about him!"

Anne chuckled. "Both he and Lady Margaret, the King's Mother may look as sour as Spanish lemons even when they are happy, but they both enjoy sweet food. That is why Henry's teeth are black. I am glad *I* do not have His Highness' cravings! I like my teeth!"

Elizabeth suppressed a laugh at that, although it was inappropriate to jeer at one's monarch, much less his saintly mother! But it was true, neither smiled overmuch, and both were reputed to love marrowbone puddings and pastries filled with currants, sugar, and cinnamon.

"Here we are." The two women and their attendants were approaching the famous abbey with its soaring façade. Presenting at the abbey gate, a monk ushered the escort into a side chamber, while the prior guided the ladies to Cheyneygates, the Abbot's lodgings. On silent feet, they proceeded through the half-built Jericho Parlour, with its dark, linenfold panels and puns on John Islip's surname enshrined in the window glass—an 'eye' and a 'slip' of a branch. Finally, they entered the Jerusalem Chamber, passing beneath an ornate letter R painted for the doomed King Richard II, in whose reign the room was built. At the far end, the Abbot awaited their presence at a cluttered desk filled with rolls and scrolls.

John Islip was a stocky man of about forty years, although he bore the air of someone much older. He was a little stout around the middle, as was common among monks. The enforcement of the old, austere rules of St. Benedict had declined in many orders, and the Abbot and the brothers ate three meals a day, full of fish, poultry, bread, and ale. Lots of ale.

He rose as Elizabeth and Anne drew close to the desk. "Dowager Duch, Lady Anne, I am pleased to receive you into Cheyneygates. Would you sit?" He gestured to two chairs by the wide, broad-mantled fireplace sporting a vivid façade of heraldic shields.

Anne and Elizabeth sat down in silence. The Abbot leaned forward on his desk, his hands placed flat on his paperwork. His expression was kind enough but also slightly bemused. "I received your missive, Lady Anne. I understand the Dowager Duchess has some concerns about the recent re-ordering of the abbey for our sovereign's eventual resting place?"

Anne nodded. "Yes, and I am sure you are aware of why that is. Duchess Elizabeth's daughter lies within St. Erasmus's Chapel and has done so for over a score of years. It seems this chapel is precisely where the King intends to rebuild."

"I have heard nothing about His Grace's plans," Elizabeth interjected. Her hands were tight and sweaty on the rosary beads she always wore on her girdle. "Surely the sanctity of the old graves will be respected. My daughter died as a princess; her husband was our Queen Elizabeth's own brother…"

John Islip coloured a little, his heavy jowls reddening. He looked uneasy and seemed a little tongue-tied. He cleared his throat, making a grating noise that set Elizabeth's nerves on edge. "I know of no better way for you to envision King Henry's plans than to see the workers in action. Follow me."

The Abbot left his house and proceeded through the cloister with Elizabeth and Anne. Entering the abbey, they walked down to the crossing, the circle of Kings and the ornate chantry chapel of Henry V upon which words were blazoned—*Henry, Hammer of the Gauls, lies here. Virtue conquers all. The fair Catherine joined her husband in 1437. Flee idleness.*

Stained and fine grisaille panes in the windows above allowed in light of varying colours, speckling the silver and gold gilded faces of long-dead monarchs—a mingling of warriors, lawmakers, and builders. Beyond the circle, the Cosmati tile floor put in place by Henry III and his wife Eleanor of Provence gleamed in swirls of green serpentine and purple porphyry, set with rich royal blue, turquoise, cerulean, and deep red glass. Brass letters ran across it, forming three inscriptions.

Elizabeth squinted, trying to read the words as she passed by.

"The inscription tells of the end of the world, Duchess," said Abbot Islip. "A hedge lives three years, a dog nine, a horse twenty-seven, and a man eighty-one if he is fortunate. The end date of time is calculated based on the lifespan of various beasts. The 'macrocosm'—see the word there?" The Abbot pointed to one section of the lettering. "That is the world in which we dwell, while 'microcosm'," he gestured to another segment of writing, "refers to man. The spherical globe mentioned above is the earth itself, bearing the hues of the four elements of fire, air, water, and earth."

He smiled, full of forced jollity. "But fear not, my Ladies, the reckoning of the learned is that the world shall last for many thousands of years yet…though, of course, this might be wrong and Christ return to judge both the quick and the dead much sooner. As it is written in Thessalonians, he will come as a thief in the night."

Islip gestured for the ladies to proceed, walking further down past the Confessor's elaborate shrine, where Elizabeth bowed her head for a brief moment, in remembrance of Anne Neville, who lay buried near the shrine's door, although without a grave marker as her husband had followed her so quickly to the tomb.

Now the mood of the abbey changed. There were few monks to be seen, but many builders and their apprentices. Hammers rang out, echoing through lofty vaults with an almost hellish clangour that was at odds with the beauty of the rest of the building. Elizabeth peered anxiously at the entrance of St. Erasmus' chapel, where two young apprentices, covered in stone dust, were manhandling a large statue.

Pulling away from Anne and Abbott Islip, she rushed into the chapel. It was in disarray—statues pulled down, ornate stone traceries smashed, stones pried apart. Chisels and other tools lay strewn around, as well as sundry boxes and torn-down wooden panels. The only thing that remained complete was little Nan's tomb, a solid chest of Purbeck marble with her name and titles written on the stone. The window above let through a sliver of light to stroke the dusty surface.

"Duchess, I bid you be careful." The Abbot bustled into the chapel with Anne Montgomerie. "It is not safe where the King's masons are working."

"You invited us here, Abbot." Elizabeth looked him straight in the eye. "There must have been something you wanted me to see. Or is it that you could not tell me the truth—hence I had to witness the destruction of my daughter's resting place for myself?"

"Would you have believed it otherwise? But I wanted to give you some comfort that, as yet, her grave is untouched."

"But soon it won't be; that much is clear, Abbot. What are the King's plans? I am just an old Dowager, locked away in the Minories…he does not talk to *me* about such matters. I am from the past—a past he would rather not think about, I gather."

It was a bold thing to say, brazen even, and possibly dangerous, for Henry was a suspicious man who had spies everywhere, even among the most unlikely of his subjects.

Despite his closeness to the King, Islip was unruffled by her harsh words. His voice held compassion. "All of St. Erasmus's chapel will be completely dismantled, and sadly, that will include the Duchess Anne's tomb. The renewed Lady Chapel shall house only the remains of those from the new House of Tudor."

Elizabeth forced back emotion; this was terrible news, but perhaps not as bad as she feared. "And the King will move Anne to another place in the abbey?"

Now he looked slightly shame-faced, staring down at his sandalled toes. "I fear not, my Lady. I did query it when he revealed his plans, thinking I might need to find a new space for her. But he said perhaps it would be better for her coffin to be exhumed and sent to the Priory of Our Lady of Thetford, where her ancestors are entombed. I know the prior, Robert Weting, and can write to him if you wish…"

"No…*no!*" Elizabeth cried, and Anne came over and put a steadying hand on her arm.

"Elizabeth, you cannot win this battle," her friend whispered. "Please, come away. I will see that proper arrangements are made for the coffin's transportation to Norfolk. You won't have to do…"

Elizabeth flinched free of Anne Montgomerie's grasp, and clutched her friend's arm. "No, listen to me, Anne. I do not want to send Nan to Norfolk…away from me. One joy I have had while living at the House of the Minoresses is that I knew my child was buried close to me. I felt I could watch over her always, guard her in death. Now they want to tear her from me. Again!"

"Elizabeth, I beg you to calm yourself. Your distress will change nothing and hurt no one but you."

"No, that much is true. But I want my daughter close to me; do you not understand? I know that if the King decrees she is moved, I am in no position to argue but perhaps…perhaps…" A hopeful gleam filled her dark, damp eyes.

"What, Elizabeth? What are you thinking?"

"The new abbess of St. Clare's, Alice Fitz Lewes, seems kindly and of generous spirit. What if I ask permission for Anne's coffin to be reburied in the convent? Surely, she would agree. It is such a little thing. *Anne* was such a little thing…"

Her tears of long-bottled grief fell then, and her friend comforted her as best she could, while Abbott Islip stood by, head bowed, unable to look at her, unable to offer any comfort, spiritual or otherwise.

"If you ask Abbess Alice, I will stand with you," said Anne at length. "I am sure a re-interment can be arranged. As you say, the Abbess is of generous temperament."

Elizabeth pulled away from Anne and turned abruptly to the Abbot. "If I make my own arrangements, will your master, the King, agree to them? Or is he insistent that my child's bones be thrust into an abbey far from London, far from memory, as if she were a tainted creature, unworthy to lie near kings?"

"I am sure he would not be averse to your plan, madame," the Abbot mumbled. "He may well be pleased, as the removal of the coffin will cost him nought."

Elizabeth stared at the man, disgust in her eyes. How could he serve such a master, so mean that he would resent paying for the body of a child whose grave he destroyed to lie in decent rest elsewhere?

"Good. I will petition Abbess Fitz Lewes about having the coffin brought to the House of the Minoresses."

The Abbot sighed. "You likely think me a fool and a villain, Duchess, but I assure you I am neither. I just want what most men want: peace and stability. If his Grace the King can bring that to England after all the years of strife, I will follow him no matter his personal failings. I hope you might one day understand." A shadow passed over his face, and suddenly he pointed to a simple, long wooden box, similar to an arrow case, thrust into a corner of St. Erasmus' chapel amidst torn-out fittings and chunks of broken stonework. "At least your daughter has not ended up like *that*."

"What is it?" asked Elizabeth, frowning. She stepped towards the box.

The Abbot cleared his throat. "Dowager Duchess, I pray you do not look. It is not a sight fit for ladies' eyes. In Henry's construction plans, several tombs had to be destroyed for his own monument to fit in. The humble wooden coffin you see holds the remains of a Queen, Catherine Valois, wife of Henry V, that noble warrior...and King Henry's paternal grandmother."

Elizabeth and Anne both recoiled in horror. "What? She is left lying there like a discarded doll?" gasped Anne. "Why is there not a decent coffin to hold her or a banner of her royal House to cover her poor bones?"

Abbott Islip shrugged. "None are privy to the minds of Kings, is that not so, Duchess Elizabeth, Lady Anne? So it has always been and, I fear, it always will be." He glanced up at the fading light in the window high on the side of the chapel. "Ah...the hour grows late; Nones draws close. I must ask for permission to return to my duties. Forgive me if I have brought you further grief, Duchess Elizabeth. It was never my intention, but I did feel you should see for yourself what changes are taking place and know that you must not expect too much from his

Grace. When Henry's mind is on the founding and flourishment of his dynasty, all else is pushed to the side. So it is with all Kings."

Elizabeth turned to leave, as Anne tried to take hold of her elbow. "No, wait!" Suddenly she pulled free and ran back into the chapel, striding between the stunned builders, who stared in amazement to see a noblewoman marching through such a place of chaos. The gruesome reredos of St. Erasmus' martyrdom had been removed, but a statue of the Virgin still stood near the altar, its head wreathed by a golden corona. It had not yet been swept away in Henry Tudor's rebuilding, and around the statue's feet, dozens of tapers still flickered. She picked one up, shielding the flame with her hand, uncaring of the heat that burnt her palm, and strode over to little Nan's tomb.

She swept one hand across the top, brushing away the dust that had gathered there during the chapel's destruction, before placing the candle down on the heavy stone lid.

"A light," she said, "to guide my daughter back to me."

Abbess Alice Fitz Lewes was sympathetic to Elizabeth's cause. "There is a small crypt below the church choir that may be adequate," she said. "It was built not long ago to hold the blessed dead, but there have been no burials yet. It lies near the place you requested for your own eventual interment, Duchess, which may even make it more suitable for the coffin of Princess Anne."

Grateful, Elizabeth nodded. She had written her will a few years ago, when she began to feel the ills of age falling heavy upon her. In it, she asked that she might be buried close to Anne Montgomerie, a true friend throughout the years. Now she would have Nan with her too—close but not sharing the same vault.

"It is fitting," she said, "that my daughter has a vault to herself, Abbess. After all, she was a Princess, even if for only a little while."

"Indeed," said the Abbess, "and it is truly an outrage that this move has been forced upon you. I will leave you to the arrangements of bringing the body hither; you may do so without delay."

Elizabeth and Anne Montgomerie went into the solar of the big house in the Close. The other noblewomen were waiting, eager for news; earlier, Anne had told them the reason she was visiting Bishop Islip with Elizabeth. They clustered around the Duchess—women who had suffered, who were unfortunate, whose husbands or kinsmen backed the losing side and now were dead. They listened to what she told them and commiserated, bringing wine for Elizabeth to drink to steady her frayed nerves.

"You know why he has done it," said Mary Tyrrell, still raw from the recent execution of her brother, James. "It is not merely to show off the wealth of his new fledgling dynasty. St. Erasmus' chapel was built by *her*…the old Queen, Elizabeth Woodville. The King wants to sweep away anything she put there."

"But that is madness—she was his wife's mother!" cried Jane. "He even restored her titles when he took the throne."

Anne's lips compressed. "Look what happened afterwards, though. Something was amiss during the troubles of 1487. No one knows exactly what. A rumour was put about that the King was unhappy with his mother-in-law because she had made a truce with King Richard and allowed her daughters to go to court. What kind of fool would believe such ridiculous falsehoods? It had been several years since that took place and Richard was long dead. Why this sudden, delayed outrage? No, this tale was a cover for something else, but who knows what? In any case, Henry sent the Dowager Queen packing to Bermondsey Abbey to dwell there as a lay boarder. Had it put about that she had grown 'weary of the world,' but that was a lie too—Elizabeth Woodville had just taken out a lease on part of Cheyneygates a few weeks prior. She did not go to Bermondsey, a house of monks, of her own volition—and now, in destroying the chapel, the King is wreaking final revenge for whatever she did to enrage him."

Bess Brackenbury cleared her throat. "Let us not forget too that Elizabeth Woodville had planned to be buried in St. Erasmus' chapel rather than Windsor. Even ten years ago, long before a single stone of his new chapel was laid, Henry would not permit her burial here. When she died, she was poor as a pauper and sent in a boat to Windsor by night with only one of Edward's bastard daughters to accompany her meagre coffin on its journey."

"By disinterring the remains of my daughter," interjected Elizabeth, who had mostly remained quiet during the conversation, "he is also removing a tie to the House of York within Westminster Abbey. Who within a generation shall now know that my daughter Anne Mowbray ever lived, or her ill-fated husband, Richard of Shrewsbury? And that is, I deem, exactly how the King wants it."

The women all fell silent then, and the shadows of evening stretched into the solar. "Light the candles," Elizabeth ordered the servants who entered the chamber to prepare for the night. "Let us chase away the darkness that has fallen. What is life if there is not one small flame to cling to, one small glimmer of hope—even if that hope lies beyond the confines of our fallen, mortal world?"

She smiled, her visage in the glow of tapers and rushlights careworn and no longer fair as men accounted it, but somehow transformed, filled with a peace and inner beauty that went far beyond mere flesh.

I deemed my Pearl was lost and dead:
But now she is found, I will hold her fast,
And dwell with her ever in the wildwood shade,
And love the laws that Our Lord has made.

The archaeologists and historians at the Museum of London were in a state of agitation. Sombre-faced, they sat in discussion in one white-painted room, lounging on uncomfortable chairs, drinking copious cups of tea. In the lab next to them, the coffin of Anne Mowbray stood open. Her tiny body lay on an examination table, decently covered, awaiting the next round of tests.

"Well, today is the day we find out if we can finish the analysis of Anne Mowbray's remains," said Dr Limehouse. "It's going to be debated in the House of Lords this afternoon. The Duke of Norfolk is still upset; he has made it very clear that he's displeased that *any* examination at all has taken place. Several other collateral descendants have expressed similar opinions. They see it as desecration of an ancestor, the issue made even worse because the deceased is a young child."

Another man, brown-suited and scholarly in appearance, with his fair hair slicked back cleanly against his head, shook his head and emitted a long, frustrated sigh. "Such a loss for science. Where has all this prissiness come from? It wasn't so long ago that antiquarians and their friends were going into the tombs of royals and nobles and doing what they jolly well liked with scarcely a whimper from any distant descendant. They carried off Edward IV's long brown hair by the handful, bits of poor old Katherine Parr and Catherine of Valois, and even drank the grave fluid found in the lead coffins at Farleigh Hungerford, thinking it might enhance longevity. Ugh. Now that *was* beastly behaviour."

Dr Limehouse nodded. "It's even more galling because the current Duke of Norfolk is scarcely related to Anne Mowbray. She had no children, of course, nor did she have brothers or sisters. The Howards became the Dukes in 1483. They were related to the Mowbrays, who are still around to some degree but not in anything like a straight line. Anne's branch of the family tree…" The older man made a deliberate cracking noise with his knuckles. "Her branch was snapped off just like that."

"I could have done without the sound effects, Dr," said the younger with a shudder. "It makes me think about how badly Anne Mowbray's lower bones were all jumbled up and damaged after those workmen up and ripped that coffin out of the ground using a chain."

"They didn't know any better, Alan. Hadn't a clue about the importance of what they'd found. Pity they hadn't contacted the museum first." He reached for his teacup, drank the milky liquid with a slurp. "Who made this? It's too weak. Dreadful."

Alan's pale, rosy cheeks grew red; clearly, he'd been the maker of the unsatisfactory brew. Quickly, he changed the subject. "Will we, do you think, have time to run further tests on the remains?"

Dr Limehouse sighed deeply, his shoulders slumping. "With all the brouhaha, I somehow doubt today's debate will go in our favour. No one wants to upset the old Duke any further, do they? A pity if it's decided she must be reburied without further delay. We could have learnt so much more. We'll likely never have such a chance again—studying a royal, known person—for years, if ever. I wanted to test her bone marrow and see if her blood type could be ascertained—but now?" He shrugged. "Such a shame. We can always hope common sense might rule, though; I mean, how can anyone call our investigations immoral, when across the country archaeological artefacts, including burials, are destroyed almost daily by careless digging and building works, often without any record made of the finds."

"It's heartbreaking." Alan folded his arms. "I just wish they'd make the bloomin' decision soon. Waiting is worse than not knowing, even if we don't get any extension for further tests."

In Parliament, the Lords argued the case of Little Anne Mowbray, the Princess in the Police Station, the wife of one of the infamous 'Princes in the Tower.' Was the Museum in the wrong, since they had not obtained a licence to exhume from the

Home Office? That was a 'no,' for the find was so unexpected and the coffin had to be moved for its own protection. It had also been unearthed before the Museum even became involved. But what about opening it? Wasn't that taking a great liberty, especially as the plaque on the casket spelled out the occupant's identity? That was a trickier matter; the Museum had not even realised there was no burial license, which was a serious oversight. However, the license had been applied for retrospectively once the error came to light. As for living 'family members', the burial was 483 years old, and the current Mowbrays and Howards were all 'collateral relatives' with no direct ancestry from Anne or her parents. And what about when the time came to reinter the Princess—where would the reburial take place, and would she receive rites of the Catholic faith she grew up in? The dean of Westminster had confirmed that a spot in the abbey would definitely be found for Anne, not far from her original resting place. No service was needed, as she would have had one when she was first interred.

The Lords disagreed on many things about the finding and examination of Anne Mowbray but agreed on several other points—one being that new laws must be enacted as soon as possible to protect potential archaeological sites so that situations like this would not occur again and heritage would not be damaged or destroyed by greedy developers.

They also agreed, almost unanimously, that Norfolk and Baron Mowbray were to be given assurances that Anne's re-burial plot was being duly prepared and her body readied for reinterment as quickly as possible.

The retrospective license for exhumation from the Home Office came through, much to the relief of the heads and trustees of the Museum who had begun to feel a backlash from the whole event and feared some kind of legal action against them. Recently, the press jumped on the controversy about the examination of Anne's remains, and the Museum found itself painted rather villainously in the papers, with comments implying that they had acted disrespectfully when examining the young Princess' remains.

The license solved the issue of legality in part, but there was still a problem, one that disappointed all the team of archaeologists, pathologists, and lab technicians working on the Minories find. The licence stated that investigative work on the remains was to be completed by May 15, and no procedures not already started were to take place. Anne Mowbray's skeleton was to be returned to her sarcophagus and delivered to the Dean of Westminster for reburial no later than the end of May.

Alan let out a groan when he heard the news from James Limehouse, fresh from a meeting about the ruling with the Museum board, curators, and other concerned parties. "Rotten luck, what more can I say?"

"Not much, I'm afraid. I think we all saw that the writing was on the wall. We can do nothing more with this find, except write it up. Well, there's *one* thing we'll need to do—get little Anne Mowbray ready for her second interment in Westminster Abbey."

Anne's bird-frail remains were lifted up and placed on rich, royal-blue fabric purchased from the department shops John Lewis and Courtalds. Washed and cleaned as much as possible without causing further damage, the tangle of her well-preserved hair was combed out with careful gloved fingers. Her new shroud was then sewn tightly shut, to keep her fragile bones firmly in place so that they would not move and cause further destruction to her corpse. Finally, she was placed into her original lead coffin, its dents and punctures fully repaired, and its lid was soldered shut.

A hired hearse arrived at the Museum and the coffin of the little Yorkist bride was placed within. It was a busy day in London, late May, the sun bright and only a few stray wisps of clouds to mar the blue of the sky. No one paid much attention to the sombre black car as it travelled through the swelling traffic. Taxi horns blared; pigeons flapped around shrieking tourists in

Trafalgar Square; Carnaby Street heaved with fashion-conscious teenage window-shoppers; crackly transistors boomed the hits of the day to fresh-faced teens with beehive hair who screamed in delight whenever the Beatles came on. *She Loves You! Yeah, yeah, yeah!*

The hearse arrived without ceremony at Westminster Abbey. A few tourists on the roadside stared and whispered, wondering what was going on. Borne by several pallbearers, the coffin was taken through the Jericho Parlour, where Anne's mother Elizabeth had long ago walked with Anne Montgomerie, and into the Jericho Chamber, where Elizabeth had met with Abbot Islip to find out the fate of her only child's tomb.

There in the Jericho Chamber, Anne Mowbray's sarcophagus was placed respectfully on a catafalque covered in a white silk pall embroidered with the Arms of England and other family insignias. Tall candles were lit and a bouquet of white roses, signifying her marriage into the House of York, was laid near the coffin, their sweet fragrance mingling with the scent of the tallowy candles.

She lay in state for several days while a handful of distant, collateral relatives filtered in to pay their respects to this long-dead, near-forgotten child.

Then, on May 31, following the conditions of the retrospectively granted exhumation license, little Anne Mowbray, Duchess of Norfolk, child-bride and princess, was laid to rest for the third time—in a shallow grave beneath the flagstones near the remains of Queen Anne of Denmark, the wife of James I.

A stone was laid over her, engraved with the Arms of Brotherton and the Arms of Mowbray and Brotherton impaled by those of Richard, Duke of York.

Below was written:

ANNE, Daughter of John Mowbray, Duke of Norfolk, child wife of Richard, Duke of York second son of King Edward IV was originally buried near this place. On the rebuilding of this chapel in 1502 her coffin was removed to the church of the Minoresses of St.Clare, London, on the site of which church it was discovered in 1964 and reburied here 31 May 1965.

Anne Mowbray, bride, princess, and much-loved only child could rest in peace at last.

Soon, with no more outraged newspaper stories and no scientific papers ever published about the results of the examinations on her bones, little Anne Mowbray fell out of memory yet again, save for the rare mention in archaeological or historical circles with specific interests in the Middle Ages and the Wars of the Roses.

A few visitors to Westminster glanced down at Anne's new memorial slab before hurrying off to investigate the more grandiose monuments in the abbey, Elizabeth I and Mary I, Henry Tudor and Elizabeth of York in gaudy splendour, just as Henry had desired, and the 17TH-century urn that was reputed to hold the fragmentary remains of Edward V and Anne's little husband, Richard of Shrewsbury (but probably in truth contained the bones of Roman or Iron Age boys…or maybe even girls.)

But mostly they just walked over her.

One night the abbey's charwoman entered the Henry VII chapel, pushing her buckets and mops on a trolley; the click of its wheels on the flagstones the only sound inside the vast building. The world outside—the fast-fleeting cars, the night buses, the overhead planes going to Heathrow or Gatwick, seemed immeasurably distant, as if on a different planet.

May Bowers did not mind doing the night shift after all the day's tourists had gone. She did not find it eerie or uncomfortable wandering among the tombs of the famous dead. It was peaceful here, and sometimes she even found herself talking to the effigies as if they were living people. She'd never seen a ghost in the abbey and never expected to, because, quite frankly, she didn't believe in them. If there were ghosts, she would have expected years ago to have a visit from her late husband, Bill, who had died while fighting in Normandy during the War. Or her daughter, Theresa, who had died of measles at just six years of age, less than three years after her dad.

Suddenly she heard an unexpected sound, which startled her and made her stop in her tracks, one hand gripping the handlebar of her cleaning trolly. When she was at work, the most she ever heard was rain or wind battering the abbey's windows and towers, or the odd shout or loud street noise that managed to pierce the thick walls.

This noise was different. It sounded…like a child's laughter. Could a child have hidden away in the abbey for a prank when it closed that day? You never knew with the children of today. So disobedient some of them…

She took a step in the direction of the sound—an area on one side of the Henry VII chapel. Walking around the impressive, yet garish, gilded tomb of the first Tudor King and his wife, she peered around cautiously and saw…*nothing.*

Then the sound came again, right there in the chapel and yet, strangely, *not*. It was almost as if she heard an echo of a laugh. For the first time, her heart began to beat fast and hard against her ribs. She thought of her lost daughter, Theresa, and how, when she died, she had prayed for months for a sign from heaven to let May know she was all right. Sometimes she felt as if Theresa had been in the room, watching. But that was only the effects of grief, she knew that now—the fancies of a bereaved woman who'd lost both husband and only daughter.

The laugh, if it truly was a laugh and not some strange distortion of sounds from outside, did not repeat a third time. The glorious vaults above seemed strangely lighter now, airy. There was a scent hovering in the air—candles? Roses? It was hard to tell, for that, too, was vanishing rapidly.

"Oh, what a funny turn that noise gave me," May whispered to herself. "The hair stood up on the back of my neck! Well, I won't let such silly notions take hold—I had best get back to work and then have a nice cup of tea."

She sloshed her mop about the inside of her bucket, clattering it almost deliberately as if trying to drown out any more unexplained noises. Humming the old wartime song, *We'll Meet Again*, she began mopping the abbey floor with gusto.

Then stopped.

Something was lying on the floor on top of the understated stone that marked Anne Mowbray's third burial.

She bent to pick it up, holding it carefully between her workworn thumb and index finger.

It was a pearl, pure and matchless, without a spot.

For what you have lost was but a rose
That flowered and faded, blossom and leaf,
But now 'tis a Pearl of price, hid close
In a casket free from rust or grief.

The Unknown 'Pearl' Poet, late 14thc

AUTHOR'S NOTE:

'The Princess in the Police Station' slightly deviates from my other stories in the MEDIEVAL BABES series about lesser-known medieval women. For one, it partly takes place in the 20th century, secondly it is in third person instead of first, and thirdly the 'princess' of the title may be the main focus, but she is not the main character, who is Elizabeth Talbot, widow of John Mowbray, Duke of Norfolk, and the sister of Eleanor Talbot, the possible secret wife of Edward IV. The medieval section of the story is seen mainly through Elizabeth's eyes.

There were a few things in my research that were rather eye-opening. I did not realise initially that Anne Mowbray had been buried in Westminster Abbey and that Henry VII had ordered the destruction of the chapel in which she was buried to make room for his lavish tomb. Henry gave no permission for her to be reburied in the abbey, so her mother Elizabeth, now residing with the nearby Minoresses of St. Clare, claimed her daughter's coffin and reburied it in the convent church. Even more surprising was finding out that the chapel of St. Erasmus in Westminster was actually intended to be the final resting place of Elizabeth Woodville, not Windsor, where her husband Edward IV chose to be buried. A recently found royal grant for St. Erasmus' chapel states 'prayers should be sung around the tomb of our consort' (Elizabeth Woodville). If Elizabeth did expect burial in Westminster Abbey, she did not receive it—her body was sent to Windsor in a mean coffin with only one mourner, Edward's illegitimate daughter, Grace.

As for Elizabeth Talbot, Anne's mother, it is thought she was buried in a crypt near her daughter's. Her coffin has never been found…

The poem that threads through the story is, of course, the famous 14th century Middle English poem, Pearl, a glorious piece of medieval alliterative verse. I have modernised and retranslated it for easier reading.

In the 20th century sections, most of the people are real (except for the cleaner at the end who is a product of my imagination!) but I have given them new names to protect the privacy of those who may still be living and/or their families. As I have no way of knowing their true thoughts or feelings about the find, I felt it was fairer to make the characters semi-fictional. I am sure you will be able to find out who the actual people involved were, if you are really interested!

JP Reedman, May, 2024

OTHER BOOKS BY J.P. REEDMAN:

RICHARD III and the WARS OF THE ROSES:

I, RICHARD PLANTAGENET: THE PREQUELS. Richard's childhood and youth. 3 books

I, RICHARD PLANTAGENET. 3 book series. First two are Richard's life from Barnet to Bosworth; the third is a tie-in about Henry Stafford, the treacherous Duke of Buckingham.

BLOOD OF ROSES and SECRET MARRIAGES— Edward IV's battle for the throne and his tangled love life!

WHITE ROSES, GOLDEN SUNNES—Collection of short stories about the life and times of Richard III's family

SACRED KING—Historical fantasy novella about the afterlife and return of Richard III in a Leicester Car Park.

WARS OF THE ROSES SHORT STORIES—short series set during the Wars of the Roses. Both Lancastrians and Yorkists. Margaret of Anjou and Henry VI, Richard III timeslip, The Duke of Gloucester's not to merry Christmas, Edward of Middleham, Francis Lovell

MEDIEVAL BABES—A series of novels on lesser-known medieval noblewomen and royals:

Eleanor of Provence, Rosamund Clifford, Eleanor of Brittany, Katherine, illegitimate daughter of Richard III, Mary of

Woodstock the Merry Nun, Juliane illegitimate daughter of Henry I, Mabel de Belleme the poisoner, Countess Ela of Salisbury, The Other Margaret Beaufort (mother of Henry Stafford), Dangereuse the grandmother of Eleanor of Aquitaine, and Matilda, wife of Henry I

ROBIN HOOD:

The Hood Game-

3 book historical fantasy series set in a Sherwood full of myth and magic.

STONEHENGE/PREHISTORY:

THE STONEHENGE SAGA—A novel of the Bronze Age incorporating the Arthurian myths.
SWORD OF TULKAR—Historical fantasy set in/around the British Bronze Age.

FANTASY and FOLKLORE:

MY NAME IS NOT MIDNIGHT
Dystopian YA fantasy set in an alternate world Canada.

A DANCE THROUGH TIME
Isabella falls through the stage in a derelict theatre and into an alternate world London where she meets the mysterious Sir Augustus Stannion. He wants to marry her, but what are the dark secrets of his stately home?

BETWEEN THE HORNS—Collection of humorous short fantasy stories set in the mythical Middle Lands between the mountains called The Horns. A land of child-eating witches, Krampuses, erl-kings, talking skeletons, flying pumpkins, and giant hares.

IN A SILVER SEA—A linked series of short stories based on British folklore. St Endelienta, St Melor of the Silver Hand, King Dunmail, the legend of Crooker and more.

TALES FROM TARA TO TIR NAN OG—short Celtic tales retold, mostly Irish but also from other Celtic countries. ANCESTORS- An American girl seeks out her genetic ancestry in Ireland and meets the Sheela Na Gig. No twee leprechauns here. Folk horror. SMOKE FROM THE SAMHAIN FIRES-4 Samhain related retellings including Crom Cruach. Plus others!

UK AMAZON LINK TO AUTHOR PAGE:

https://www.amazon.co.uk/J-P-Reedman/e/B009UTHBUE

USA AMAZON LINK TO AUTHOR PAGE:

https://www.amazon.com/stores/J.P.Reedman/author/B009UTHBUE

.

Printed in Great Britain
by Amazon